Malik's eyes were drawn to the woman lying on the gurney, her eyes wrapped in heavy white bandages.

Long auburn hair framed her face like a halo, and one of her smooth, bronze-colored arms rested peacefully at her side. The other was bent at the elbow and covered by a pink cast. The rise and fall of her chest were the only signs that she was alive. Her body was long and slender and he immediately had the vision of a tall, shapely woman with the legs of a dancer. She was incredibly beautiful, and instinctively, his heart went out to her.

"Car accident," the orderly said. "She's doing much better than when she was first brought in. Right Ms. Daniels?"

Kennedy did not respond, hating the fact these people were talking about her as if she were some laboratory rat devoid of distinguishable feelings. Statements like the orderly's reminded her in no uncertain terms that, all in all, she was lucky to be alive. Of course, none of these people were living the physical and emotional hell she was living, but they still held the uniformed opinion that she should be grateful....

Books by Kim Shaw

Kimani Romance

Forever, For Always, For Love
Soul Caress

Kimani Arabesque

Pack Light
Free Verse
Love's Portrait

KIM SHAW

is a high school English teacher in New Jersey and has
enjoyed creative writing since she was a child. She resides
with her husband and two children, enjoys reading and
volunteering and would like to become a world traveler.

SOUL
Caress

KIM SHAW

KIMANI
ROMANCE

KIMANI PRESS™

ISBN-13: 978-0-373-86035-7
ISBN-10: 0-373-86035-8

SOUL CARESS

Copyright © 2007 by Kimberly Sharrock Shaw

www.kimanipress.com

Printed in U.S.A.

Dear Reader,

When I wrote this novel, I was thinking about the many hopeless romantics who have the courage to love despite differences, distances and demographics. That's not an easy thing to do at a time when there is so much strife and violence in the world around us. However, somehow love manages to endure.

Malik is every man. He is the brother who may not have the most education, money or prestige, but what he has is strength of character. Even though Malik suffers from the same self-doubt and faltering esteem that many people suffer from, he still finds the courage to live an honorable life and to love his woman the way she deserves to be loved. Through her determined love for Malik, Kennedy is made strong enough to expose and denounce the prejudices of her family. Let them be an example for us all.

Coming up next is little sister Madison's story, which promises to be just as passionate and captivating. Thank you for your continued readership.

Yours truly,

Kim Shaw

"Where there is love there is life."
—Mahatma Gandhi

Chapter 1

Kennedy gently pushed her favorite compact disc of all time, Wynton Marsalis's *All Rise,* into the vehicle's CD changer. Instantly, the quiet car was filled with the soulful wail of a solitary trumpet. Nothing else in this world spoke to Kennedy's weary spirit after a grueling day at work like Wynton's artistry. She could always count on his music to massage her senses and transport her to a serene place.

She turned the knob of the wipers so that the blades moved faster across her car's windshield. The driving rain made it difficult for her to see more than five feet on the sleek black road ahead. It had been raining without pause for the past two days, the skies wrapped in foreboding darkness night and day. Although, even if there had been brilliant sun, Kennedy would not have known it. She spent all of her daylight hours in the office for the past two weeks. Nestled against the butter-soft beige leather of her Mercedes Benz sedan, Kennedy attempted to relax and to will her body to release the day's tension. She did not regret the fact that she had been pulling down long hours at Morgan Stanley, and while it was a major coup for a second-year analyst to be second in command on a client as prestigious and world-renown as Otman Hotels, it was the most mentally and physically exhausting challenge she'd ever faced. She couldn't help but snicker with self-satisfaction, however, as she counted the zeros on the huge bonus that would be waiting for her at the end of the deal. She'd had her eyes on a piece of investment property and now was the perfect opportunity for her to buy something for herself without the help or interference of her parents.

Kennedy was no stranger to hard work. She'd always been driven. As far back as she could remember she had been striving to be the best. In the first grade, she'd built a volcano for the science fair. She hadn't been able to rest until she could make the thing explode and spew hot lava three feet into the air. Twenty years later she showed no signs of lightening up. A laundry list of things to do loomed ahead of her in the coming weeks. Between the Otman deal at work and assisting with the planning of her parents' thirtieth wedding anniversary celebration, she had a lot on her plate.

Right now all Kennedy wanted to think about was the hot bath she planned to take as soon as she got home. She couldn't wait to curl up with the latest Eric Jerome Dickey novel as she sipped a glass of Merlot.

The crunch of shattering glass was the last sound Kennedy heard. One minute she was driving down the slick asphalt of King Street, just a bit over a mile away from her two-bedroom duplex in Falls Church, Virginia. Suddenly, the tires of her car skidded and to no avail, she pumped the breaks, attempting to regain control. Her brain raced as she tried to remember the things you were supposed to do to avoid a wreck, yet everything seemed to be happening faster that her recollection could keep up.

The car entered into a forty-five mile per hour spin and Kennedy gripped the steering wheel, the skin taut across her knuckles. The last thing she saw before her eyes closed and her grip on consciousness fractured was a flash of lightning that zipped across the sky.

The sleeping beauty caused quite a stir at the otherwise quiet Annandale Hospital that night. It was a Tuesday evening and emergencies had taken a break for a while. As she was wheeled into the trauma center, the doctors and nurses sprung into action, determined not to lose her. While all patients received the same dedicated care at Annandale, there was something about the almost lifeless woman, whose regal beauty was still apparent even in her unconscious and battered state, that tugged at their core, causing adrenaline to surge throughout the emergency room. Her skin was burnished bronze, and her slim curvaceous figure was captivating even in crises.

Evening gave way to night as the medical staff fought to restore her. In the wee hours of the morning, shortly before dawn, Kennedy awoke from the car accident feeling as though her skin were on fire. Every inch of her 5'9" frame hurt as every muscle seemed to be torn to shreds. She attempted to open her eyes but found them tightly bandaged with a thick and endless stream of gauze and tape that had been wound securely around her curly, matted hair and throbbing head. She tried to lift her right arm, but discovered that it had been set in a cast, weighing it down and rendering it immovable. Her left arm remained under her control, but as she lifted it, a searing pain shot through her shoulder and followed a path directly to the very core of her brain.

She lay still for several minutes, her mind blurry and confused. The air held a sickening smell that was a mixture of blood, which was caked in her nostrils, and antiseptics. Nothing made sense to her, as though she were in a vacuum of suspended time and space. For a moment, she considered remaining there, lost and unknowing. Yet soon panic filled her, as her mind raced to find its way out of its solitary confinement.

Feeling as though she were trapped inside of a horror movie, Kennedy's fear mounted steadily until she began to scream in her mind at first and then attempting to let that scream out. Her voice was initially barely a whisper. Her lips felt like they were twice their normal size as she slid a thick sandpaper tongue across them. She swallowed the stickiness coating her throat and tried again. With each attempt her voice grew louder, changing from a whisper to a cracked, strangled sound. She tried again and again until finally there came a loud piercing wail of agony.

The intensive care unit door burst open and all of a sudden Kennedy's room became a mass of activity. Doctors and nurses charged in and began talking all at once, or so it seemed to her confused mind. Kennedy tried her best to make sense of what they were saying as they checked her over, reviewed her vital signs, removed, replaced and tightened bandages, but it was as if they were speaking Greek.

"Kennedy…Kennedy Daniels, I'm Dr. Moskowitz. Ms. Daniels?" a deep voice called, reaching her ears from a distance it seemed.

The voices asked her a myriad of questions, wanting to know if she knew her name or could tell them where she was. Kennedy answered slowly, trying to be as coherent as she possibly could. Each word was painful to articulate, her burning throat and vocal chords refused to cooperate with her. She knew the day of the week and the date. She recited her name and date of birth. She was even able to provide an oral history of her day, right up to Wynton Marsalis and the drive home. Everything after that was a mystery to her.

She begged and clamored for them to tell her what had happened to her. When the clatter in the room finally died down, all but one of the voices faded away.

"Kennedy, I know this must all be very confusing and upsetting to you, but I need you to try to calm down," the stranger said soothingly.

He introduced himself again as Dr. Moskowitz, head of emergency medicine, and advised Kennedy that she was no longer driving toward her home but in fact at Annandale Hospital. She was in the intensive care unit where a team of doctors and nurses had been working through the night to take excellent care of her.

Kennedy could hear his voice but nothing he said made any sense to her. All she could think was that none of this could possibly be happening to her.

"Kennedy, we've contacted your family…the

police found their phone number in your cell phone…they're on their way," Dr. Moskowitz said.

Kennedy could feel the doctor's hands on her, cold hands that checked her pulse again. While Dr. Moskowitz's voice was soft and composed, his hands felt rough against her bruised skin as he touched her.

"Kennedy, you are one fortunate young lady to have come out of that car wreck, and let me reassure you that you are going to be okay."

By the time the doctor departed, his confident words that her prognosis for a full recovery remained fair ringing in the air, Kennedy had begun to scream again. This time the anguish resonated on the inside, her voice reverberating against the walls of her brain. A heaviness settled in the pit of her stomach like a boulder at the bottom of a creek. She cried a river of tears that soaked her bandages as she prayed for God to make what was happening not be happening to her. However, it was definitely real and she never felt more alone, or more vulnerable in her entire life than she did at that moment. The once fiercely independent young woman cried like a baby for her mother to come and kiss the pain away.

Chapter 2

Kennedy's parents, Dr. and Mrs. Joseph Daniels, along with her sister, Madison, arrived at the hospital late in the morning following the accident. They imperiously descended upon the intensive care unit and demanded the full attention of the hospital staff. Joseph Daniels quietly, yet firmly requested that the doctors treating his daughter be paged and sequestered for a meeting at once. His wife of thirty years, Elmira Ellington Daniels, stood by his side, apparently used to watching her husband take command.

"Oh, dear Jesus," Elmira bellowed upon seeing Kennedy as they entered her room.

Elmira crumpled against the stout frame of her husband. Kennedy was stirred awake by the unmistakable sound of her mother's smoky voice. She turned her head in the direction of the noise and immediately felt the smooth, beefy hands of her father wrap themselves around one of hers.

"Elmira, calm down. She's going to be fine," he said reassuringly. "Sweetheart, can you hear me?"

"Yes, Dad," Kennedy croaked, her throat still hoarse and hurting.

Suddenly, Elmira was overcome with sobs and, without the ability to see her mother, Kennedy was sure she was dramatically fanning herself to ward off one of her infamous fainting spells. Right on cue, Joseph issued a familiar phrase.

"Elmira, you don't look very well. Why don't you go outside for a while? Have yourself a cup of coffee or tea," he added. "I saw a café right near the security desk in the lobby."

Kennedy was used to scenes such as this one, but for once she was just not up to playing her part in it. Joseph and Elmira had a perfunctory marriage in which the pampered Elmira was shielded from any discomfort or uneasiness. Kennedy had fallen into the habit of echoing Joseph's sentiments in many instances. This was not one of them.

"Yes, I suppose you're right," Elmira said in a reluctant tone that was worthy of an Oscar award.

Elmira rose from her perch at the side of

Kennedy's bed. She smoothed the front of her brown tweed flare-legged pants. At fifty-two years old, Elmira Daniels looked more like a pampered celebrity than a housewife, married to a cosmetic surgeon. Today's designer outfit, pantsuit, chocolate-brown patent leather platforms and handbag, was what could be called dressing down for her. Her attire alone could be priced at over three thousand dollars, and that figure tripled if one were to assess the four-karat pear-shaped diamond ring set in platinum, the two-karat diamond earrings or the solid gold watch on her dainty wrist. Kennedy inhaled her mother's signature scent and the familiar feeling was both comforting and disturbing.

Elmira's thick wavy hair was cut in a short bob, shaved in the back circa 1986 Anita Baker, dyed dark brown with blond highlighted bangs sweeping her forehead. The only sign revealing her age were the tiny crow's-feet visible near the outside corners of her hazel eyes. That minor flaw was no match for the meticulously applied cosmetics in which she lived. Her buttermilk complexion was as beautiful today as it was when she was half her present age. Her face wore a dual expression today, the first of which was concern for her eldest child. The second expression—slightly masked, yet apparent to those closest to her—spoke to the indignation she felt that such a tragedy could have befallen one of the Daniels.

Madison rolled her eyes, sickened by her mother's constant dramatics and her father's characteristic indulgence. If Kennedy could respond in the same manner, it was no doubt that she would have because as solicitous as her sister was, today's behavior was extreme.

"Hey, sis, are you hanging in there?" Madison asked, moving closer to the side of the hospital bed after Elmira exited the room.

"Maddie? Yeah, I'm okay," Kennedy lied.

Kennedy's heart warmed at the sound of her sister's high-pitched voice. With the aid of the pain medications she'd been given, which had the effect of making her mind a fuzzy place where happy images of her life rested, she fondly remembered when Madison, three years her junior, had first begun to talk in complete sentences. The family had been certain that she'd grow out of her voice or that the highness of her tone would deepen as she got older, but it never really did. Kennedy used to tease her when they were little, telling her she sounded like a cartoon character. Madison, never one to care what people thought of her, would giggle and imitate Minnie Mouse. As Madison grew older, every part of her changed and developed except the tone of her voice. That voice set her apart from the other girls and the boys flocked to it and to her like kittens to warm milk. Madison learned to use her voice, and all of her other attributes, to get the things she wanted. She was shorter than Kennedy, closer to her mother's height at only about five-seven in heels. Her complexion matched Elmira's, while Kennedy had inherited a shade closer to their father Joseph's golden-brown skin tone. The sisters shared the same high foreheads and wide, dimpled smiles, making it clear to anyone who saw them that they were related despite the other physical differences. If there remained any doubt that they were sisters, those doubts were silenced when anyone attempted to mess with one or the other.

One hot summer day when Kennedy was nine years old and Madison six and attending Elko Lake sleepaway camp for the first time, Kennedy had been down near the lake with the older campers, learning how to build a raft out of bamboo and vine, when all of a sudden one of the kids from Madison's group ran down yelling that Madison was getting jumped by a group of campers. Kennedy took off before the words were fully off of the girl's tongue. She ran uphill, around the cluster of cabins to the arts and crafts area. Through the storm of dust that was being kicked up, she saw three girls surrounding Madison, a sea of arms and hair tangled together. Madison was holding her own against the trio of troublemakers, but she was in a no-win situation, especially since one of the girls was big, bucktoothed Liza, who was the size of two six-year-olds put together.

Kennedy snatched one girl from the back of her head and literally tossed her through the air, the girl landing in a loud thud five feet away. She grabbed Liza by one arm, spinning her around to face her and before the girl knew what was happening, Kennedy had clocked her in the jaw. Liza's hands went up to protect her face and Kennedy seized the moment, raising her Pro-Ked-clad foot and kicking the girl in the abdomen as hard as she could. Liza dropped to the ground like a sack of potatoes. Kennedy looked over her shoulder and saw that, now that Madison was in a fair fight, there was nothing to worry about.

Madison had her last opponent on the ground and was a whirlwind as she sat on her knees wailing on the girl's upper body and face. The first girl Kennedy had attacked was sitting on the ground holding the spot on her head that was oozing blood from where it had struck the side of one of the craft tables when Kennedy had tossed her. Liza attempted to get up and Kennedy took that as a sign that she hadn't received enough of an ass-whipping. She pounced on the girl, her fists balled, seeking to teach her never to mess with a Daniels again. By the time the counselors were able to separate and subdue Kennedy and Madison, all three of their victims were blubbering mixtures of blood and tears. From that day on, wherever they went, the story followed them and it was a rare brave soul who'd even think about confronting one of them.

In recent years, Kennedy had felt as though her once inseparable relationship with her sister had grown distant. The older Madison got, the more she rebelled, while time had the exact opposite effect on Kennedy. Madison seemed to get pleasure out of going against their parents' wishes, rocking the boat as turbulently as she could. It put a strain on the camaraderie she and Kennedy once shared, as Kennedy was the one who followed their parents' instructions to the letter. At twenty-five, Madison had become wild and impulsive and she heeded the advice or words of caution of no one, including her onetime ally, big sister Kennedy.

Seeing Kennedy bandaged from head to toe and lying in a hospital bed having nearly escaped death, obviously paused Madison. She quickly swiped at the tears that were swimming on the rims of her eyes, turned up her dazzling smile and stroked the only space on Kennedy's face that didn't seem bruised, bandaged or purple with pain.

"That's good to hear. Girl, for a minute there I thought you were trying to leave me alone with that crazy woman!" Madison joked.

"Maddie," Joseph warned, although he secretly got a kick out of his youngest daughter's ability to ruffle his wife's feathers.

"Come on, Dad. I sat behind you guys on the flight down here and all she did was talk your ear off the whole time about going after the manufacturer of Kennedy's car. Then what'd she say? Oh yeah, she thinks somehow the state of Virginia is responsible for this. As if something they did or didn't do to the roads caused Kennedy's accident. I am surprised she doesn't want to sue Mother Nature for the rain. I swear, she is a piece of work," Madison fumed unapologetically.

Joseph held his tongue, unwilling to go toe to toe with his daughter, especially when she was speaking the truth.

"Madison, don't upset your sister," was all he said.

"Oh, Dad, there's nothing I can tell Kennedy about *her* mother that would shock her."

She had taken to referring to Elmira as only Kennedy's mother as the two of them argued more and grew ever more distant. Kennedy's attempt at a laugh came out as a wince as the ever-present pain intensified. Madison called for the nurse, who came in and turned the dial on the machine that released morphine into Kennedy's system intravenously. Madison sat silently, holding her sister's hand while sleep overcame her.

Joseph looked on for a few minutes and then slipped out of the room to go and tend to his wife. Madison shook her head, keeping her thoughts to herself. For the remainder of that day, while their father returned periodically to sit in silence near Kennedy's bed, their mother could not bring herself to return to the room. Madison knew that her dis-

comfort came more from the unwillingness to
accept that one of her children could possibly have
a permanently damaged face and distorted body
than any other reason their father tried to gesticu-
late. In the world of Elmira Daniels, there was no
such thing as imperfection.

Chapter 3

Kennedy spent days in and out of consciousness, flying high on pain medication. As she slept, her dreams were filled with images of twisted metal and broken glass. The sounds of her screams combined with the whining screech of tires on wet pavement reverberated in her brain despite her desperate efforts to escape them. She held the taste of blood in her mouth and each time the pain relievers dissipated from her bloodstream, her bones ached and her skin stung as if she'd been dipped in acid. When alert, in the moments before a new dose of medication took control, Kennedy tried to remain positive, praying for the will to grow stronger.

Her parents and Madison were staying at a Hilton Hotel about ten minutes away from the hospital. Madison jokingly whispered to Kennedy when they were alone, that while their parents loved her very much, there was no way Elmira would be caught dead in the Best Western directly across the street from the hospital. Kennedy laughed for the first time since the accident.

"It's so good to hear you laugh again, sis. Dad and I went to the auto body shop to check on your car. I hate to tell you this, but it's totaled."

Madison laughed when Kennedy groaned at her news.

"Hey, look at it this way—the fact that you walked away from the twisted wreckage of that car, figuratively, anyway, is a miracle. Let's just count our lucky stars. Besides, when you get better, we'll squeeze Daddy to buy you a cute little Aston Martin."

Joseph, Elmira and Madison stayed by Kennedy's bedside in shifts for the first few days. Kennedy's emotions were split between feeling an overwhelming need to have their presence at all times and wishing she could have a few moments alone, without her family, doctors or nurses surrounding her. This experience taught her that a hospital beat a mall for most crowded, hands down.

"What happened to her?"

Kennedy heard a deep voice rise above the usual hospital noises, but she lay still beneath the white blanket. It was very early in the morning and her family had not yet arrived for the day. She was being returned to her room after having a CAT scan performed, the second since her accident. The doctors were attempting to rule out any possibility of injury to the brain that may have gone undetected when she was first examined.

Malik Crawford was working with a transport team from Stillwater Rehabilitation Center. They were at Annandale picking up a patient who was being discharged and delivered to Stillwater for continued care. Their patient, a wealthy magazine editor who'd suffered partial paralysis from the waist down as the result of a skiing accident, was waiting to receive discharge papers from his doctor.

Malik had gone down to radiology to say hello to a buddy of his while he waited and was now waiting for an elevator back upstairs. His eyes were drawn to the woman lying on the gurney, her eyes wrapped in heavy white bandages. Long auburn hair framed her face like a halo and one of her smooth bronze-colored arms rested peacefully at her side. The other was bent at the elbow and covered by a pink cast. The rise and fall of her chest was the only sign that she was alive. Her body was long and slender and he immediately had the vision of a tall, shapely woman with the legs of a dancer. She was incredibly beautiful and instinctively, his heart went out to her.

"Car accident," the orderly said. "She's doing much better than when she was first brought in, right Ms. Daniels?"

Kennedy did not respond, hating the fact these people were talking about her as if she were some laboratory rat devoid of distinguishable feelings. Statements like his reminded her in no uncertain terms that, all in all, she was lucky to be alive. Of course, none of these people were living the physical and emotional hell she was living, but they still held the uniformed opinion that she should be grateful.

"Her leg looks like it's positioned a little too high…this can't be very comfortable for her," the voice said.

Genuine concern echoed in his words, as if he felt somehow responsible for her comfort and care. She wondered if he were a hospital worker.

Kennedy felt a strong hand under the bend of her knee. As the metal bar above the gurney from which her broken leg was suspended was adjusted, bringing her leg about ten degrees lower, she concentrated on the softness of the wide palm against her skin. The warmth from his touch remained on her leg after he removed his hand.

"Godspeed on your recovery, Miss," the voice said, just as her gurney began rolling off of the elevator.

The sincerity in his tone struck her, yet still she offered no response. She felt the urge to say something to the man but was still so far from being sociable that she couldn't make herself talk. She was thankful, however, because she did feel more comfortable after his adjustment. His voice stayed with her, its soothing timbre ironically finding its way into her soul when the pain was at its worst.

Five days after the accident Kennedy was removed from the intensive care unit and transplanted into a private room. The fire in her skin had all but vanished by then and slowly she had begun to feel sensations other than the raw pain that had been her constant companion since the accident. The nurses and orderlies settled her into her new room with all of the machines and tubes still connected. When they left, her head and eyes still bandaged and taped shut, Kennedy believed that once again she was alone. She had grown accustomed to not being able to see anything through the thick bandages and had begun to learn to listen for sounds of life around her. Suddenly, she heard breathing and turned her head sharply in the direction from which it came.

"Why didn't I think to bring a camera? Darling, you look positively wretched."

The voice came from a corner of the room.

"Skyy?" Kennedy cried.

"It's me…in the flesh," Skyy answered, moving to Kennedy's bedside and plopping down on the bed next to her.

She took Kennedy's non-bandaged right hand in hers.

"I would have been here sooner, sweetheart, but would you believe there was not one empty seat on one stinking plane until last night?"

Skyy leaned down and pressed cool lips against the side of Kennedy's cheek.

"How are you?"

"I'm feeling a lot better than I look, I'm sure," Kennedy answered weakly.

"Mmm, hmm. Well, my dear, judging from the slur in your voice, I'd say you've made friends with the Percocet fairy. That's probably why you're feeling so good." Skyy giggled.

"Actually, it's Vicodin now and we are on a first name basis," Kennedy said, a pained smile pushing through her lips.

Skyy and Kennedy had been best friends since seventh grade at the all-girls boarding school they'd attended. They had been more like sisters than friends ever since they'd been paired together as lab partners in biology class. In a social circle that consisted of the Who's Who in Young Black America, Skyy was the most real person Kennedy had ever met.

Unlike most of Kennedy's other friends, and herself for that matter, Skyy was not part of a legacy of doctors, lawyers and social debutantes. Her father was a self-made man who had made friends with the right people, and clawed his way into a brotherhood of the moneyed folks of North Carolina. No matter how hard he tried, however, there was lingering in him, his wife and their only child, an element of roughness of the Southside of Chicago, from which they had fled as soon as he could afford it when Skyy was twelve years old.

While Skyy adapted to their new lifestyle of Bentleys and private schools, she never accepted or adopted the arrogance of the wealthy. When she and Kennedy first started hanging out together, Kennedy had attempted to draw her into her circle of friends, who were the prettiest, most popular of the girls, both black and white, in school.

Seated in the cafeteria enjoying chef-quality meals of broiled salmon and steamed asparagus tips, the girls were whispering and teetering over one of the new additions to the school, a girl who was there on scholarship, whose hand-me-down outfits and GAP jeans made her stick out like a sore thumb amongst the rest of the Lacoste-wearing, diamond-studded young girls. Skyy had remained quiet, studying the girl who sat alone, eating her lunch beneath the cloud of adolescent snubs. All of a sudden, Skyy rose from her seat, picked up her tray and marched deliberately across the cafeteria. She stopped at the girl's table, said something to her and then sat down. Kennedy and her crew were stunned and after that day, Kennedy had been told in no uncertain terms that she had to make a choice. It was Skyy or them. Today, she turned to face her friend's voice, glad at the choice she'd made.

"Where are your folks?" Skyy asked, tossing her hair over her shoulder.

Kennedy wished she could see Skyy, wondering what transformation her friend had gone through during her latest jaunt overseas. Skyy had been in Italy for the past three months. The firm she worked with, Samage Designs, had landed one exclusive hotel or restaurant after the other and Skyy's fresh eye and youthful approach to design was a large part of the equation. Travel was the thing that, once bitten, Skyy had yet to be able to shake. She loved packing up and hitting the road and for her, the farther the distance, the better. Before Italy, she'd been home in North Carolina for only a couple of months, having spent the prior nine months in Japan designing and implementing the construction of a five-star hotel in Tokyo.

Each time she came back to the United States, Skyy was a different person. Once, there was a short, fiery red hairstyle, that, despite the shocking effect it had, actually looked fantastic on her. Another time, after a visit to India, she came home with her head shaved bald. These days, her hair having grown back to her shoulders, she rocked a permed layered style, colored jet-black. Her copper-penny brown face, with its slanted eyes and pixie nose, was sun-kissed and vibrant, bespeaking her strict vegan diet and rigorous exercise regimen.

"They left yesterday. Daddy had to get back to his patients and Mother, well, you know Mother. She can't stand living out of a suitcase," Kennedy laughed.

She didn't need to let on to Skyy that she was glad that her parents had gone back home. Having them around worrying over her was as intense as the physical discomfort she was in, if not more. Skyy knew better than anyone how trying Kennedy's parents could be.

"What about Maddie? What's she up to?" Skyy asked.

"You know Madison…nothing new there. She was here, too, and was fighting with Mother as usual. Once I assured them that I was going to be fine, she hopped in her car and headed up to New York to visit Liza Penning."

After the young Daniels sisters had kicked Liza's butt all over the summer camp that year, Madison and Liza had become best friends. Liza was now a stand-up comedienne living in New York City.

"I'm sure Elmira was thrilled about that," Skyy laughed.

"Yeah, well, what can she do? Madison is a grown woman now."

"Yeah, grown and still living at home, sponging

off of Mommy and Daddy. I don't know why your parents don't just cut her off. I bet you that would make her straighten up and fly right."

Kennedy considered Skyy's words for a moment, and one moment was all it took for her to dismiss them. First, there was no way her parents would ever cut Madison off. The Daniels would walk through hell with gasoline cans strapped to their backs before they ever allowed one of their own to have to make do without or depend on others for their survival. Secondly, as much as Madison rebelled against them, she and Elmira were so much alike that not accepting her and her behaviors would be the equivalent of her mother turning against herself. No, Madison had yet to find that thing, if it existed, that would push her parents to the breaking point, although she'd come very close once or twice.

"She promised that she'd stop back in to check on me by the weekend. If you're still here, maybe you can talk some sense into her."

Both Kennedy and Skyy erupted with much-needed laughter at the absurdity of that one.

"Yeah, well I'll still be here by the weekend, but I damned sure won't waste my breath talking to your sister about anything other than shoes and men." Skyy smirked.

Skyy stayed in town for the remainder of the week, spending the days seated by Kennedy's bed-side, reading to her. They finished the Eric Jerome

Dickey novel Kennedy had been planning to read before the accident, as well as a half a dozen gossip magazines and the latest issues of Ebony and Essence magazines. They listened to the news on television every evening and the daily talk shows in the afternoon. Skyy fed Kennedy the nutritious, yet tasteless hospital meals that were delivered three times a day, and snuck in cheesecake and other sweets in between meals. It was also Skyy's job to deliver the twice-daily medical updates to Elmira and Joseph, who threatened to fly back up to D.C. in a moment's notice. At Kennedy's request, Skyy kept them at bay with glowing reports of the patient's progress.

Kennedy was, in fact, improving. The bruises on her skin had begun to scab over and peel away. She could now move her left arm without feeling any pain, although she was somewhat limited by the full arm cast extending from the center of her right hand up to her elbow.

Her shattered right knee was still held immobile, sealed tightly in a cast made of fiberglass and hanging from a trapeze above her bed. Skyy gave Kennedy a French pedicure, after sponging and applying lotion to her size nine feet. She did the fingers on both of her hands to match, trimming and shaping the nails first. Finally, she made her way to Kennedy's hair, using a sponge and the aloe-scented latherless shampoo she'd purchased at a local beauty supply store. She combed the once glowing mane, freeing it of its tangles and dry patches where various liquids had settled since the accident. Carefully avoiding the bandages that were wound around the nape of her neck and across her forehead and eyes, Skyy parted Kennedy's hair into small sections and wiped the shampoo through. Next, she brushed it until it began to shine again, braided it into a long, tight French braid and wrapped a ponytail holder securely around the end.

She helped Kennedy change out of the ugly blue hospital gown that had been placed on her damaged body by the nurses into a pale pink, Victoria's Secret nightshirt made of pure silk.

"Now, you're beginning to look human again," she remarked when she had finished her spa treatment.

"What do you mean?" Kennedy exclaimed.

"Girl, I hate to say this about my one and only best friend, but you were extremely torn up when I got here. Crusty, ashy and wild don't even begin to describe the way you looked," Skyy replied.

As much as Skyy rejected the attitude of the bourgeois black class to which her parents wholeheartedly subscribed, she did appreciate the finer things in life. She was a woman of taste. The standards she set were high, but they were her own. She believed a woman should look her best at all times, but rejected the belief that good looks could only be achieved with a lot of money.

"Oh, great Skyy. Way to kick a sister when she's down," Kennedy lamented.

The hardest part of the past week had been the fact that she didn't have the use of her eyes. She couldn't wait until the bandages were taken off so she could get a good look at herself—her body and her injuries. From touching her face, she could tell that it was no longer swollen and with the exception of the gash on her forehead, which the doctor had told her had required twelve stitches to close, there were no other injuries to her face.

Skyy had told her that the bruises to her arms and legs, as well as the scratches that had come from the broken glass, were all healing well. Despite this, she longed to see herself for herself. She was impatient for the moment she could look into a mirror, stare into her own eyes and confirm that she was really all right. She needed to see for herself that she had really made it through the worse ordeal of her entire life. However, she'd have to wait a few days longer. The ophthalmologist had conferred with Dr. Moskowitz, reviewing the initial X-rays and optical images taken of her eyes. They agreed that Kennedy's eyes simply would need time to heal and that no medical interventions were warranted.

As promised, Madison returned to D.C., although it was Sunday afternoon when she finally made it back down from her jaunt in New York City. A mere ten minutes in her presence and Skyy shook her head dismally, excusing herself from the room. The next day, with Madison on the road again, headed home to North Carolina, Skyy finally voiced what had been eating away at her brain.

"Kennedy, I hate to be the bearer of bad news, but your sister is headed for a fall. Now, let me know if I'm overstepping here, and I'll just shut my mouth."

"Of course you can say whatever you have to say, Skyy. You know you're family. And, if I don't like it, I'll just curse you out…like family." Kennedy smiled.

"I just don't understand why your parents allow that girl to rip and run, not working or going to school…doing whatever the hell she wants. She looks like crap and she dresses like a five-dollar hooker."

Kennedy winced at Skyy's words, but every part of her told her that they were true. Skyy was the one person in this world who she could count on unequivocally to tell her the truth, no matter whether she wanted to hear it or not.

"Does she get high?"

Skyy's question was raised in a tone that suggested that she already had her own beliefs on the matter.

"I think she's dabbled a little in the past, but I don't think it's heavy. I mean, you know that Liza girl she hangs out with and the rest of those spoiled rich kids playing artists up there in New York they associate with."

"Well, she looks like she's doing more than dibbing and dabbing. Look, girl, I know you've got enough to deal with here, getting yourself healed and whatnot. However, the next time you go home to Carolina, I suggest you sit that girl down and have a talk with her. She needs to get her butt back into school or something constructive and in a hurry. She's too old to play the rebellious teen role. It isn't cute anymore."

Madison had dropped out of Spelman College after her first year. This had been especially shocking since she had begged her parents to allow her to go there, although they had expected her to follow in Kennedy's footsteps and attend Princeton.

They'd relented, unable to deny the fact that although Spelman was a historically black university—and in their minds accessible to all types of people who were of questionable backgrounds—it had graduated countless successful African-American women of high caliber and social standing. When Madison had returned home after her freshman year, having maintained a low B average, and announced that she wasn't going back, it was puzzling. It eventually occurred to Kennedy that the only reason she'd wanted to attend Spelman in the first place was to piss her parents off and now that the thrill of that was gone, she was ready to make a fast exit.

Madison had spent the past three years *finding herself,* whatever that meant. From Kennedy's standpoint, all she'd managed to find since leaving

Spelman was more and more trouble for her parents
to bail her out of.

First it was the apartment she begged them to
rent for her, and then was summarily kicked out of
after breaching the complex's rules with wild
parties and unregistered overnight guests. Then
there was the time she was detained in a jail cell in
Mexico after getting into a bar fight in Cozumel,
Mexico, with the daughter of an elected official. Her
father had paid dearly to make that little indiscre-
tion disappear. The girl blew through more money
than a category five tornado through Kansas in the
height of storm season.

Kennedy agreed with Skyy, promising that as
soon as she'd recovered enough to travel, she'd head
home to spend some quality time with her baby
sister. In the meantime, she had to concentrate on
getting herself out of that hospital bed. The sooner
she got on her feet, the better off she'd be. When
Skyy finally left, planning to make a quick pit stop
in North Carolina to see her parents before returning to her work—and the distinguished Italian gen-
tleman she was dating—in Rome, it was a tearful
farewell. Each woman realized how much they
relied on their friendship and the truth of the matter
was that they had come very close to losing that, had
Kennedy's accident been worse than it was. Skyy
left with the promise that she'd be back in another
couple of months to check on her girl.

Chapter 4

Kennedy spent the days convalescing in solitude. The thought of having visitors, other than her parents, her sister and Skyy, sent her into an unexplainable panic attack. She received a dozen bouquets of flowers from coworkers at Morgan Stanley, from her parents' bridge partners, the Thompsons, and from her condo neighbor, Victoria, with whom she occasionally shared a cup of morning coffee over their adjoining balconies. The cards, the flowers, the phone calls all wishing her well, were appreciated, but after only a few days, she could not take any more. She wanted to be left alone, to wallow in self-pity at the unfairness of it all. While

Kennedy was not the type of person who stayed down for long, she felt like she deserved some quality time in *melancholyville*. She reasoned that after a good, uninterrupted dose of the *why me*'s, she could concentrate on the business of getting better and healing her body and mind.

She had the phone, which her parents had turned on in her room, turned off again and asked that visitors be refused by the hospital staff. Anyone who called the nurses' station to inquire about her recovery was directed to call her parents. In the days that passed after Skyy left, Kennedy replayed the accident over and over in her mind, kicking herself for not having had her brakes checked weeks before when they'd first begun squeaking. She questioned why she had been driving so fast, headed home to an empty apartment and a book. She tried her hardest not to cry, not wanting to soak the bandages that still covered her wounded eyes. Yet the morose thoughts that clouded her mind brought with them a deluge of tears that struggled against her sealed eyelids.

The nurses and doctors checked in on her regularly, poking, prodding, changing bandages and recording her progress. Two weeks to the day after the accident, Dr. Moskowitz, conferring with ophthalmologist Dr. Pitcher, informed her that it was time to remove the bandages that sealed her eyes and to perform a comprehensive examination of her vision.

Both doctors had cautioned that there might be some damage to her vision, although they remained optimistic that the scratches that were observed immediately after the accident were superficial. Kennedy's excitement and anxiety were at odds within as she prepared herself for the unveiling. Her hopes remained for the best, as she was more than ready to get out of the hospital and get back to her life.

Kennedy sat impatiently in the cushioned chair while Dr. Moskowitz slowly snipped away the bandages round her head. As he unwound the strips of gauze, he talked to her in a soothing voice, explaining what he was doing each step of the way. As the layers of gauze diminished, Kennedy anxiously awaited a glimmer of light or her first sightings. Anything that came into view would be welcomed after residing in darkness for so many agonizing days.

"We taped your eyelids down to help with the healing," Dr. Moskowitz stated as if in answer to Kennedy's thoughts.

Finally, when all of the bandages had been removed, Dr. Moskowitz prepared to peel back the thick adhesive that kept Kennedy's eyes closed.

"Before I take away the tape, I just want you to be prepared for changes in your vision. There may be blurriness or distortion. The corneas may not be completely healed yet. I don't want you to be alarmed. Just relax and describe to me what you are able to see as things come into focus."

The tissue around her eye sockets felt sore and Dr. Moskowitz reassured her that this was due to the fact that the lids had been held shut and bandaged for so long. There had been no damage to the bone or tissue surrounding her eyes. Kennedy took a deep breath as Dr. Moskowitz glided a wet piece of gauze across both of her eyelids to moisten the adhesive. Then he quickly pulled away the tape, freeing first the left eye and then the right. Kennedy took another deep breath to steady her racing heartbeat and slowly opened her eyes. The ever-present darkness that had surrounded her for the past two weeks remained.

"Dr. Moskowitz?" she called, her voice a whisper. "Dr. Moskowitz?"

"Yes, Kennedy. I'm right here. What can you see?" he asked.

"Nothing. Dr. Moskowitz, why can't I see you? Everything is dark and...blurry."

Kennedy reached both hands outward, her palms slapping against the doctor's chest. Her breathing became rapid as panic seized her heart. Her fingers groped until she made contact with the doctor's lab coat. She clutched the fabric harshly, pulling at it.

"Kennedy, Kennedy. Calm down, please. I need to examine you," Dr. Moskowitz said.

He pulled a small penlight from his breast pocket, shining it into Kennedy's eyes, first the left and then the right. Her pupils remained wide and unseeing, save for blurred shadows of objects around her. Not one thing was discernable to her eyes and there existed only the most minimal snatches of light.

"Kennedy, it is too early to determine anything concrete about your vision. You have to remain optimistic. These things sometimes take more time and patience than we'd like them to."

Further examination showed that the deceleration of her brain during the crash had caused Post Trauma Vision Syndrome. The prognosis was mixed and it was uncertain if Kennedy's sight would ever return.

Tears pooled in Kennedy's brown eyes instantaneously, engulfing her sockets and sliding down her honey-brown cheeks. Dr. Moskowitz suspended his examination and attempted to comfort her with words that fell upon deaf ears. She could not hear anything nor could her mind register a coherent thought. She had awakened from the singularly most harrowing incident of her life and despite the pain and anguish, had sincerely believed that with time, things would get back to normal. Now, the realization that nothing would ever again be normal for her smacked her in the face and she crumbled from the weight of the blow.

Chapter 5

"Bonjour," Nurse Crosby beamed as she burst through the door to Kennedy's private room.

Her shoes squeaked as she crossed the carpeted floor, bustling toward the window. Nurse Crosby snatched the curtains back in one quick motion.

"There. Let's let a little sunshine in here," she quipped. "That's better, isn't it?"

Kennedy did not respond nor did she move. She wanted to ask what difference it made whether the room was sunlit or not. It wasn't as if she could see it. Curtains open or closed, the room was still a dungeon devoid of color and light. She didn't say this, however. There was no reason to annihilate

Nurse Crosby's cheery disposition with her sour one. Besides, she'd rather sulk silently in her stew of despondency.

"It's a beautiful day out there, Ms. Daniels. What do you say I help you get ready for your walk?" Nurse Crosby asked, as she pulled back the blanket that covered Kennedy's lower body.

Kennedy leaned forward abruptly.

"Walk? I'm not going for a walk," she replied.

Obviously, Nurse Crosby had had one too many cups of caffeine this morning. Either that or Kennedy surmised that she was as blind as Kennedy was if she couldn't see that, not only was Kennedy's leg up in a trapeze with a cast from foot to thigh, but that she could not see her hand in front of her face. There would be no walking today.

"Of course you are, dear. This is a rehabilitation facility, you know, and we certainly can't get you back up on your feet if we leave you lying on your backside all day. Now, one of the client assistants will be by in just a few moments to take you out to get some fresh air. He'll escort you all over the grounds. Just wait until you see the place. It's to die for. Oh, Stillwater spared no expense when it came to landscaping this beautiful property. Just you wait."

By now Nurse Crosby had removed the hooks that had kept Kennedy's leg suspended one foot off of the bed. She carefully lowered Kennedy's leg until it rested on the bed. Kennedy listened to the squeak of her orthopedic footwear as she moved away from the bed toward the bathroom. Kennedy listened as the nurse ran water into a basin, turned off the faucet and squeaked her way back to the bedside.

"I've brought you a warm wash towel so that you can wipe your face. Here you go."

Kennedy reached out, moving her fingers tentatively in front of her until she touched the towel. She grabbed it, bringing it to her face. When she was finished, Nurse Crosby took it away from her.

"Here is your toothbrush. The paste is already on it."

Kennedy felt in front of her again until she located the toothbrush and clumsily directed it to her mouth. She brushed her teeth for several moments and then took the cup of water offered by Nurse Crosby. She rinsed, gargled, spit into the basin and rinsed again.

"Now, that's better. Once you've had your wheelchair lessons, you'll be able to do this in the bathroom all by yourself. Won't that be great?"

Kennedy slumped back against the pillow without responding. It was taking every ounce of reserve that she possessed not to go off on the nurse. Normally, she was not what you would call a combative person. She hated conflict and discord, preferring to find less confrontational ways in which to work out disagreements. Unless she felt backed into a corner with no alternatives—as in the case of

the rumble at summer camp back in the day—
Kennedy was mild-mannered and diplomatic. Her
patience was running low these days, however, and
the last thing she was prepared to deal with was an
overzealous nurse who'd swallowed one too many
happy pills.

"Do you feel like pink or blue today?"

"What?"

"Pink or blue? I've taken the liberty of making
two selections from your closet—the first is a blue
denim dress and the other is a pink skirt and
matching sweater. What will it be?"

"I don't care," Kennedy responded tersely.

"Well, let's go with the denim."

Without another word Nurse Crosby helped
Kennedy remove her gown and slip into the denim
dress. After her arrival the day before, she'd been
left alone pretty much to rest until evening, when
another nurse had helped her bathe in a special
shower designed for people with casts on their legs.
Within the shower stall there stood a metal closet
in which Kennedy placed her plastered leg and then
the nurse closed it, thereby keeping it sealed and
protected from the water.

"All right, dear, I've got other clients to tend to,"
Nurse Crosby announced as if Kennedy had been
keeping her there.

Kennedy listened as the nurse retreated, closing
the door behind her. She covered her face with her

hands, pressing her fingertips against her useless orbits. She cursed and muttered, allowing herself to release the frustration that she'd held in check while Nurse Crosby was in the room. While Kennedy's other injuries had begun to heal, her emotional health teetered on the brink of crumbling. Her arm had been freed from the cast and despite a slight loss of muscle tone, it felt as good as new to her.

Outwardly, she had mended sufficiently enough so that the doctors at Annandale were comfortable in signing her out of the hospital and sending her to Stillwater Rehabilitation Center to begin the arduous task of rebuilding her life. However, inwardly her spirit remained fractured and she felt no motivation to even get out of the bed. The fire that had previously driven her to become the lively, energetic woman that everyone who knew her believed her to be, had been extinguished.

She took sharp, deep breaths, feeling as though she were suffocating under the unfairness of it all. She gasped for air where there was none to be had.

"Good morning, Ms. Daniels. I'm Malik Crawford and I work the day shift here at Stillwater. I've been assigned to work with you during your stay."

Kennedy turned toward the door, the direction from which the baritone voice came. Two things struck her at precisely the same moment. One, the voice was vaguely familiar, although she could not place it. Secondly, whoever he was, the brother had the sexiest voice she had ever heard in all of her twenty-eight years. She wiped the tears from her cheeks, momentarily pulled from the cliff of crushing despair on which she had been lingering.

"Mr. Crawford—" Kennedy began.

"Malik, please. Just call me Malik. As I said, we'll be working together during your stay. I will take you to all of your therapy sessions, doctor's appointments and twice-daily trips outdoors. Outside of that, if you need anything else…if you'd like to leave your room, say, to go down to the game room or something, I'm your man. Okay? Just buzz the nurses' station and ask them to page me. How's that sound?"

I'm your man sounded interesting, but Kennedy didn't say that. Had she been in another frame of mind, another place in her life, she would have allowed the heat of attraction to spill over her. Yet other more pressing things were on her mind, like the fact that she was dependent on this person for however long she was at Stillwater. Dependence was not something she did very well. She was used to taking care of herself and coming and going as she pleased. Once again, the realization that she was no longer the woman she'd once been smacked her in the face. Once again, she fought the powerful urge to cry.

Malik watched Kennedy for some reaction. He'd neglected to tell his new client that he had been part of the team who'd helped to unload her transport bed from the ambulance that had brought her to Stillwater early the day before. In part, he'd omitted this fact out of sheer embarrassment. He had been rendered speechless when he'd laid eyes on Kennedy Daniels for the second time in his life. Absent were the bruises and bandages, the intravenous tubes and the heart-monitoring devices. Gone was the poor nameless individual for whom he felt sorry.

Her jacket unzipped to reveal a white camisole that fit her torso like a glove. On her left foot she wore a pair of yellow-and-white Nike cross-trainers, and her hair was pulled back off of her face and held in a ponytail by a large barrette. Her fresh face and fit figure could easily have been that of an eighteen-year-old college freshman, yet something in her carriage even as she was rolled on a gurney out of the transport van told him that she was a mature woman in every sense of the word.

The singular thing that struck him, literally sucking the air right out of his lungs, was her smile. It had been ever so brief, but immensely potent. One of the nurses, an older woman who did a remarkable imitation of comedienne Adele Givens, said something that prompted the brief smile from Kennedy. Behind the expensive shades that covered one-third of her face, Kennedy smiled, her plump lips parting, revealing beautiful teeth and exposing a small dimple in her left cheek. Malik's iron-man persona melted, causing him so much discomfort that he'd had to excuse himself to other duties just to get away from her before he became a staring, blundering idiot.

Twenty-four hours later, Malik had collected himself. He was confident that he would be able to handle his duties with professionalism and decorum with the light of a new day around him. Upon entering her room, he'd steeled himself against the potential of her physical beauty to stir his emotions. He was not a man for whom a woman's physical appearance was enough to do more than cause a slight stir in his loins. What turned him on mentally and emotionally was a woman whose intellect and conversation were equally as attractive. If he couldn't talk to a woman and share his ideas, hopes and dreams, he could not share his body with her, either. He had no way of knowing what rested inside of Kennedy Daniels, so to him she remained just another pretty woman—a client at that.

Kennedy reached her left hand out to the side, bumping it against the side of the nightstand clumsily. She moved her hand several inches up until she could feel her way along the surface of the table. When she came into contact with the object for which she had been searching, her shades, she snatched them up gratefully and moved slowly to her face, placing the shades over her eyes. Malik, having received no verbal response from her, took that as a sign that she was ready to go. He came farther into the room, pushing a wheelchair in front of him. He stopped next to her bed.

"I know movement is a little tough for you right now with that cast covering most of your leg, but we'll help you learn how to navigate with it and trust me, as soon as you get used to it, it'll be time to take it off," Malik said.

He hadn't expected a response, although he felt that at least a nod of the head would have been nice.

"I need you to try to turn your body sideways, swinging your broken leg toward me while letting the other one hang down toward the floor. I'm right here so don't worry…I'll catch you if you need me to."

With Kennedy feeling less than trusting of Malik's ability to safeguard her transfer, the transition from the bed to the wheelchair was thorny and awkward. She laced her arm around his neck, noting how strong a neck it was, but she gripped him so tightly that he had difficulty maneuvering. By the time he got her into the seat, his breath was ragged and little beads of sweat had popped up on his forehead.

"All right, Ms. Daisy, ma'am, shall we?" Malik joked as he began pushing the wheelchair of his silent new client.

The sun felt hot on Kennedy's face. She tilted her face up toward it, allowing it's warmth to massage her stony facade. Malik stood a few paces away from her, alternating between watching her and staring at the lagoon. This was his favorite place on the Stillwater grounds for several reasons. For starters, not many people came down here as it was quite a trek from the structure. The tranquility he found here on his daily breaks was rarely broken by chatter. He appreciated alone time, since it was something that was a rarity, especially since he'd allowed his brother to move in with him earlier in the year. At the apartment, with its small two bedrooms, a kitchen that opened to the combined living room and dining area and claustrophobic bathroom, there was rarely an opportunity to find solitude. His brother, Malcolm, who was seasonally unemployed, often had the company of some female, and no matter who the pick of the week was, they all had the same annoying giggles and the same exaggerated moans, which could be heard in every corner of the tiny place.

Here on the lagoon, Malik would sit and stare at the ducks, contemplating his life. He often felt that just like those ducks, all he was doing was floating on the same body of water, day in and day out, with no progress and without change. At thirty years old, Malik had become restless and dissatisfied. By other people's accounts, including his parents, he had a good stable job with benefits and a pension that he'd only have to work thirty years to receive. All he needed to do was find a good woman, start a family and his life would be perfect. For Malik, however, there was so much more to the puzzle of his existence. The only problem was that even though he knew he wanted more for himself, he had no idea what else there was in store for him. Furthermore, he had even less of an idea of how to go about getting it.

A noise that came from Kennedy pulled him from his thoughts. From his vantage point behind her, he could not see her face, but the heave of her back and shoulders told him unmistakably that she was crying. He hesitated, unsure of whether he should leave her alone and let her cry uninterrupted or not. He knew all too well that sometimes a person just needed a good cry. His grandmother used to say that crying was like giving your spirit a bath. Still, something pulled him to her, awaking a need in him to comfort her, even though she was a complete stranger to him.

"Ms. Daniels, are you okay?" he asked as he moved in front of her.

She'd removed her shades and they lay on her lap. When he spoke, she moved her hands up to her face, covering her eyes. Her body trembled.

"Ms. Daniels, are you in pain? Would you like me to call for one of the doctors?"

She shook her head vehemently from side to side.

"No, I don't want anyone," she said.

Finally, a complete sentence from her. The sound of her voice, even though it was choked with emotion, surprised him. He hadn't expected it to sound so strong. Even though she was obviously upset, her voice held a quality of vigor that was undisturbed by her current distress. With a right hand that trembled, she slowly reached up and wiped at the tears on both sides of her face. She lowered her left hand, fingering the shades that lay in her lap. Her eyelids blinked rapidly for several seconds before fluttering to a standstill. She stared out in front of her, seeing nothing.

Malik looked at her face, for the first time seeing it in its entirety without the distraction of eyewear. His heart literally stopped beating for a moment, his breath caught in his throat. He knew that she was beautiful. He had recognized that the moment he'd rolled her out of the transport vehicle. What caught him by surprise now, touching a part of him that he had not even acknowledged in years, was the fact that despite her tears and current distress, there was a harmony of spirit that possessed her. He had never laid eyes on a woman in his entire life that made him feel like he never wanted to look at another woman—until now.

"I'm sorry," she said softly. "I just…can I have a minute alone?"

"Sure," Malik said, continuing to stare at her.

It took all the strength within for him to disengage from her face and move away from her. He walked a few feet along the lagoon and sat down on one of the large boulders that lined the edge. Occasionally, he dared to sneak a quick glance in her direction. She held her head erect, her face pointed toward the water. She didn't move nor did he. He glanced at his watch, knowing that it was past the lunch hour and that he should have her back in her room already. Yet he was unwilling to interrupt her solitude.

Although he had other duties that he was currently neglecting, he had no intentions of rushing her. He couldn't very well leave her by herself as she was a long way from the point in her rehabilitation where she could be left on the grounds to take care of herself. He knew that there was no clear prognosis as to whether her vision loss was temporary or permanent, but that the goal was to teach her how to live as a visually impaired person just in case. That would take weeks of work with the specialists and it would also have to wait until she had the use of both of her legs again. Until then, she was dependent on him and, try as he might, Malik couldn't help but like the sound of that.

Chapter 6

"Thank you for...for today," Kennedy said as Malik rolled her back to her room.

It was after eight o'clock in the evening and Kennedy had just finished an hour-long lesson in Braille reading for the blind. She was exhausted, having been kept on the go all day long. After her walk with Malik, she'd returned to her room for a quick bite to eat and then, because she was running late, had been rushed to physical therapy. There she'd spent thirty minutes learning how to pull her body upright from a reclining to a sitting position. Next was a trip to the weight room where she stretched and lifted weights for another thirty minutes. Dr. Pitcher, the ophthalmologist, came in to see her later on, where he performed a brief examination of her eyes. This was followed by dinner, another walk, or ride, depending on how one looked at it, around the grounds and finally the brail lesson, her last activity of the night.

Malik knew that Kennedy was referring to her breakdown at the lagoon that morning and while he didn't feel like he had done anything special, he appreciated her gratitude.

"Don't mention it," he said as they arrived at her room.

He opened the door and rolled her chair inside. There was a chill in the air and he moved toward the wall that held the thermostat for the central heating and cooling system.

"Should I turn up the heat a little bit for you?" he asked.

"Umm, no. I like it this way. I was a winter baby," Kennedy answered.

"Uh, oh. Don't tell me you're one of those T-shirt and flip-flop wearing, beach buffs in November kind of people. Girl, don't you know that black people are from the tropics—we ain't built for the cold weather." Malik laughed.

It happened. For the first time since she'd arrived at Stillwater the day before, or at least while she had been in his presence, Kennedy laughed out loud and directly from that place inside where people are free and unpretentious. For Malik the sound was like the ringing bells of a winning slot machine. He watched her, the way her head tilted back and her mouth opened wide. It warmed him, filling him with the happiness that comes from seeing someone else's spirit brightened, especially when that someone was special.

Malik lifted Kennedy from the wheelchair that had become an extension of her and carried her to the beige two-seater in the sitting area of the modest room. Although it was time for his shift to officially end, he did not want to leave her and he fished for excuses to hang around even if only for a few minutes more. He moved the wheelchair closer so that it was within her reach and started explaining the different mechanisms. A less than complicated piece of equipment, it was quite a task for him to stretch out his explanation, but he gave it a shot. Kneeling by her feet, he guided her hand to the wheels, across the breaks and the footrests. He let his fingers linger a second on top of hers, tantalized by the softness of her digits. A sudden knock at the door interrupted what had to be the highlight of his entire week, perhaps even month.

Jessica Hubbard, the night shift client assistant, entered. She took over where he left off, covering the clients he'd been in charge of all day. While there was much less activity at night than during the day, Jessica's job was to help the female clients shower and get settled in for the night. She was still around when many of them awakened in the morning and for those who preferred to bathe in the morning and needed assistance, she took care of them. By the time Malik arrived at eight o'clock in the morning, Jessica would have seen to it that the clients were dressed, fed and ready for whatever activities were lined up for them for the day. Together, they handled a caseload of between five to seven clients at a time and both of them felt as though they had lucked out in being paired to the same team.

"Hey, Malik, Marci told me you were still around. Running late tonight?" Jessica asked as she entered.

"A little bit. I was just trying to get our new client settled in. Kennedy Daniels, I'd like you to meet Jessica Hubbard. She's on call nights."

"Hello, Ms. Daniels. It's nice to meet you," Jessica said.

"Likewise. So you're the one I'm supposed to bug in the middle of the night if I need a drink of water or if I have to potty?"

"Yep. Feel free to bug away. Sorry I wasn't around when you got in yesterday…I had a minor family emergency. Are you about ready to call it a night? If not, I can come back in a little bit."

"Thank you, Jessica. I'm pretty beat, so, yes, I'm ready."

"Well, then. All right, I guess I'll head out now

so you ladies can do your thing. Kennedy, I'll see you in the morning," Malik said reluctantly, aware that his time with Kennedy had finally come to an end.

"Fine," she answered, acutely aware of the fact that at some point during the course of their day together, she had gone from being Ms. Daniels to Kennedy.

Later that night, surrounded by a darkness that she believed she would never become accustomed to, Kennedy's thoughts drifted to Malik Crawford. She wondered what he looked like and whether his smile came from his eyes. Did his stature match the deep timbre of his voice? What about his hair? His nose….

Chapter 7

Blindness, whether temporary or permanent, was not a condition to which Kennedy found herself able to snap her fingers and adjust to. Waking up, after twenty-eight years of living a full and functional life, to darkness, had sent Kennedy into depression. She oscillated between fighting the feelings of despair and giving in to them completely. All the time she questioned why this had happened to her. Was her current situation a result of something she'd done or some offense against nature she'd unwittingly committed?

She found herself only going through the motions of the rehabilitation regimen the doctors and physical therapists had set out for her. Essentially, she had given up on ever having anything that resembled the satisfying life she used to lead.

The team of professionals who were working to reconstruct her life included a psychologist, Dr. Goodhall. Dr. Goodhall was warm and engaging yet she asked tough questions. Questions that forced Kennedy to think about things she preferred not to dwell on. Kennedy didn't want to probe into the innermost regions of her sentiments, especially because she was struggling to hold the fragile pieces of her feelings together.

Dr. Goodhall suggested that she allow people to be her comfort and source of strength while she dealt with the difficult transitions that lay ahead. This was a suggestion to which Kennedy objected vehemently. As far as Kennedy was concerned, not her parents, other family members nor anyone could pacify her. Furthermore, she could not take one second of her mother's theatrical hysteria nor anyone's pity. She had hit an emotional rock bottom and contrary to popular belief, her misery did not want any company.

Unfortunately, being a resident at Stillwater did not afford her much solitude. There was a steady stream of staff members with whom she had to interact, countless appointments and therapy sessions and then there was Malik.

He arrived knocking at her door every morning

at eight o'clock sharp and even when she reported that she did not feel like going out, he quietly insisted that she join him. He talked as if they were going out on a date instead of out for a walk around the grounds of a facility for people with disabilities. In spite of herself, it was his subtle charm that coaxed her out of her room every day without fail.

"Malik, what do you do when you're not playing caddy to damaged invalids like me?" Kennedy asked one afternoon after Malik had parked her wheelchair off the path that led into the gardens.

"Damaged invalids?" He laughed. "I don't see any damaged invalids around here."

"You know what I mean. Let's face it, this place isn't exactly crawling with healthy people. So you do this all day long…it's got to be depressing as hell."

"Not at all. Actually, I kinda like spending time here. I mean, in this place you've got all kinds of people facing some of the most difficult challenges of their lives and many of them do it without complaint. Now take folks who have their health and the use of all their faculties out there. They curse and grumble about everything from their Starbucks not having enough sugar to a traffic light that takes too long to turn green."

Kennedy thought about what he'd said, wondering if she had been one of those people before her accident. While she didn't think that was an accurate description of herself, she did realize how much in her life she had taken for granted. She could not remember the last sunset she'd seen, having spent the past few months and years locked inside of Morgan Stanley's offices until long after dusk every night working away like any good corporate soldier.

"That didn't really answer your question, did it?" Malik grinned. "All right, well, basically I'm not a partying type of guy. So when I'm not working here, I spend time at bookstores, getting my work-out on at the gym…watching a good flick on television. That's pretty much it."

"Oh, I doubt that's it. What about dating? Don't tell me you're a monk or something?"

Malik laughed.

"No, I'm not a monk. I just don't date a lot. Bad breakup a while back, so I guess you could say that I'm just being cautious. There's a lot of nutballs running around out there disguised as Miss America, you know. What about you? I know there's got to a whole bunch of guys chasing after you like groupies."

"Groupies?" Kennedy laughed. "Hardly. It's just me, my job and, oh, can't forget about my goldfish…Lucy and Ricardo."

Malik studied Kennedy's face for a moment, noting the tension that rested there and in her neck and shoulders. In the days that he'd spent caring for her, he'd come to realize that one of her greatest flaws was also her greatest asset. She was incredibly strong and resilient, yet she had no idea how much of those qualities she possessed. She thought that she'd crumbled beneath the weight of her personal tragedy and yet all he could see was a woman who was incredibly determined to hold on to her life. Kennedy's only problem was that she believed that she could do it alone.

"Goldfish, huh?"

"Yeah, my neighbor, Victoria, is feeding them while I'm here. I might tell her to keep them if…"

Kennedy's voiced trailed off.

Malik crouched down beside Kennedy's chair and plucked a delicate white flower from the bush in front of them. He moved the fragrant blossom up, stopping just beneath her nose. When the scent reached her, she smiled, reaching out to touch it. Her hand brushed against Malik's and a warm flush coursed through his veins.

"The corydalis is one of the longest blooming flowers in the world. People look at its ferny foliage and graceful flowers and doubt its fortitude. But this is a plant that will find a home in cracks in rocks, on slopes in woodlands and along paths. After that, the corydalis self-sows wherever it can and regenerates for years. In essence, no matter what you do to this little guy, he keeps going, kind of like a certain little lady I know," he said, releasing the flower to her outstretched hand.

Kennedy accepted the flower and raised her other hand to capture Malik's fingers. As she laced slender fingers around his large hand, a slow smile formed on her mouth.

"Marci, the visual therapist, keeps telling me that there are so many other ways to see other than with your eyes," Kennedy said. "What do you think I see right now?"

"I don't know. Tell me," Malik asked, his heart caught in his throat.

"I see a man whose heart is gold and whose spirit is benevolent. I see…a very dear friend."

They sat in the garden for a while longer, each lost in a moment that was profoundly peaceful and nourishing to each of them, for very different reasons.

The days morphed quickly into weeks and without even being aware of a change in her mood and perception, Kennedy began to look forward to waking up in the mornings. Even the grueling physical therapy she endured was a welcomed part of her daily routine and she pushed herself to get stronger.

The cast was removed from her leg and replaced with a thinner, more flexible one. To her astonishment, she had extremely limited strength and mobility in that leg. Everything she tried to do hurt, including the stretching exercises that the therapist put her through twice a day for a half an hour at a time. By the time she finished working out, Kennedy was a sweaty, teary-eyed mess, but that did not deter her from coming back for more.

Instead of giving in to the desperation and hopelessness that had nearly crippled her since the accident, Kennedy had now found a dogged determination in getting better. There was no doubt that the change in her mood was partially due to Malik Crawford.

They began to spend a great deal of time together. Malik visited her during his hours on duty, as well as in his leisure time. He brought sandwiches from the deli and shared his lunch break with her, either out on the grounds or, during inclement weather, seated on the floor in her room for an indoor picnic. He knew that the unspoken rules of Stillwater stated that client/staff interactions outside of caregiving should be limited, but he could not help himself. He had seen how depressed and discouraged Kennedy was when she'd first arrived and for some inexplicable reason, he felt an overwhelming sense of responsibility to her.

Kennedy was unlike any other client he'd ever worked with or any other woman he'd ever encountered. There was a strength and inner beauty that attracted him, called out to his spirit, and he could not ignore it. Still, he knew that he had to be discreet and without saying anything specific to her, Kennedy understood the same. In the presence of others, they were client and patient. Alone, as they strolled along the winding paths or sat in her room tossing grapes into the air and trying to catch them in their mouths, they laughed and talked, sharing confidences and becoming friends.

With pride she boasted about her family and the accomplishments of her ancestors. Malik learned that Kennedy came from one of the most influential clans in North Carolina, with a staunch reputation dating back to the early abolitionist movement. He was enthralled by the way her face lit up as she shared with him stories of firsts in her family—the first black banker in a town, the first black storeowner in a city and the first black lawyer in the state. Malik couldn't help but be equally impressed by her family legacy. It also made him uncomfortable. Secretly, he wished that he had the same stories of significant successes to tell about his family tree, but he knew of no such accounts to share. His reservations were shattered, however, in the face of Kennedy's interested prodding and gentle sweetness, and he felt compelled to share what he did know about his family.

Malik's parents, Fred and Joyce Crawford, spent their careers as blue-collar workers. The Crawfords raised their family—Malik, an older brother, Malcolm, and an older sister, LaToya—in D.C.'s rough Northwest district. Malik was proud that his parents had managed to stay together for thirty-five years and counting.

While Kennedy talked about summers spent traveling abroad, Malik laughed as he remembered his summer days spent splashing around in front of the fire hydrant on the corner of his block. The more they talked, the more they realized that they had very little in common in terms of their upbringing and lifestyles. Yet they also realized that that fact made them all the more interested in one another.

For Kennedy, spending time with Malik helped her to focus on something other than the devastation the accident had caused to her life. He made her forget to find time to cry each day. He made her remember all the things that she should smile about. She found being with Malik easier than talking to anyone else, quite possibly because he did not know her before the accident. Her parents always talked about when she got better and after her eyesight came back, as if there was no room for any other possibility. They were constantly reminding her of her job at Morgan Stanley, all of her accomplishments and the bright future she had in front of her. To her, their words were an insinuation that she could control her recovery, and that they expected her to bring about a positive outcome. Nothing less would be acceptable to the Daniels.

The Daniels of Charlotte, North Carolina. Pride and familial esteem were their cornerstones. Kennedy loved who she was and where she came from, but often she had found herself questioning if her family's legacy was as defining of character as her parents had led her to believe. She'd felt like a rebellious adolescent on countless occasions when she'd secretly volunteered at homeless shelters and food banks or spent time at children's hospitals reading stories and doing crafts. These were acts that her parents, who believed that giving back could be done from afar and with a checkbook, would never approve of.

"You must be careful around whom you position yourself, dear. Certain qualities can rub off, you know, and once they do, they're hard to be rid of," Elmira had often warned.

The older Kennedy got, the more confused she grew as she tried to reconcile the beliefs that her parents had instilled in her and the ideas and reasoning taking shape in her mind. Right now, as she dealt with one of the harshest realities she'd ever had to face, the idea of letting them in with their pretentious ways and unrelenting ideals was more than she could handle.

"Sometimes I wondered if I would be a different person if I'd grown up with different parents…a different family. It's like, I don't know how much of me is really me, do you know what I mean?" Kennedy asked Malik.

"No, I don't," Malik answered honestly. "Tell me."

And so she unburdened her soul with Malik more than she had with her doctors, the therapist or even Skyy, who called twice a week from her home and then from Italy to check on her. While their conversations were filled with laughter and love, there was still a part of Kennedy that remained guarded. Skyy was her best friend in the whole world and up until the accident, she had felt closer to her than anyone else. Skyy was essentially family, but she was also a part of a time that seemed like it belonged in another life. Kennedy felt as though she had to pretend that things were going to be all right because that's what her family wanted and needed to believe. She considered that she was being unfair to Skyy, but she couldn't help how she felt.

Visits from coworkers and other associates were also taxing for Kennedy. Victoria came once, bringing Kennedy more clothing from her apartment. Trisha Williams, a fellow analyst, stopped in, bringing news and gossip from the office. She appreciated their warm wishes, but could not take their pity and expressions of compassion. It was as if they were writing her off, convinced that the Kennedy that they had known had died in that car accident. While she recognized that she was indeed a changed woman, she could not understand why people looked upon that fact as a negative thing, a reason for sorrow. Slowly, she had with gratitude accepted the fact that her life had been spared in that horrendous accident for a reason. While she had not yet been able to figure out what that reason was, she refused to continue to feel sorry for herself. So she made it very clear to visitors that she did not wish for them to return. She cited the fact that she had much work to do toward her recovery and needed to concentrate on that. She detected a profound sense of relief in her colleagues when she asked that they allow her to get in touch with them once she was released from Stillwater and had gotten back on her feet.

In contrast, her time with Malik held no demands or pressures. For the first time in her life, Kennedy didn't care what other people had to say or what they would think about her. On days when all she felt like doing was crying, Malik held her hands and let her cry. When those days became few and far between and her smile returned, lingering for longer stretches at a time, he was right there, smiling with her. There was no need to think about what she'd lost or how her life had changed, because with Malik nothing before that moment existed.

Just over a month into her rehabilitation, Kennedy was feeling particularly restless, a sure sign that she was well on the road to recovery.

"Malik, I really need to get out of here. I mean, it's been raining for two days straight and I'm tired of being cooped up in this building," Kennedy complained when Malik came to pick her up from physical therapy.

"I feel you Kennedy, but unfortunately, we're not allowed to take clients outside in bad weather."

"Come on, Malik. I've got a raincoat. Please?

Just for a few minutes...a quick roll around the grounds. Look outside...it's barely drizzling."

Malik's sense of responsibility was no match for his need to please Kennedy. She didn't even need to twist his arm because, like it or not, she had already twisted his heart. He hesitated for only a moment before wheeling her down the hall toward the back elevators. She giggled with delight when she realized that he was going to grant her wish, a sound that made any final resistance he was feeling dissolve instantly.

Outside, Kennedy took several deep breaths, inhaling the fragrant scent of moist air and flowers.

"Do you know why they say that springtime is for lovers?" she asked as Malik pushed her chair along the wet concrete.

"No, why?"

"Because it's so fresh and new, like the first time two people make love. Before they know what pleases their mate, they're just testing the waters...trying things out and everything seems like it's the first time they ever felt it."

"Spoken like a woman in love," Malik said.

Kennedy did not respond. They rolled around the back of the complex in silence.

"Have you ever been in love, Malik?" Kennedy asked after several minutes.

"Yes... At least I thought it was love. I'm not so sure anymore."

"Why not?"

"Well, 'cause when things started to go bad, it made me question if I ever really knew her. I mean, if you're in love with someone, you should know that person inside and out, right? If not, then how can you say you're in love with them?"

Malik's tone was as questioning as it was pained.

"I guess. But, you know, people don't usually let you get to know them. Not completely, anyway. They hold the real stuff back because they're afraid you won't like them if you know all about them," Kennedy said.

"Some people do that, I guess."

"Are you saying that you don't? What you see is what you get, Mr. Crawford?"

"Exactly," Malik answered. "And...I feel like you haven't held anything back from me. Right?"

"Right, but that's different. I mean, we're just friends, right?"

Kennedy's breath caught in her throat as she waited for his response.

"Right," Malik answered.

He stopped walking, bringing Kennedy's chair to a stop. There was more that he wanted to say to her, much more, but the words would not come. How could he explain to her what a genuinely nice person he found her to be and how it was an extreme pleasure to have met someone like her? He didn't want her to think he was coming on to her. Although she was unquestionably beautiful and sensuous, his attraction to her was much more than flesh and body parts. There was a spiritual magnetism between them that he had never experienced before.

As he tried to find a way to say what was in his heart, the clouds above them grew ominously dark again. Before he could formulate the words, large drops of water began to pelt them.

In seconds, the sky opened up and dumped buckets on them. Kennedy laughed as Malik raced along the winding paths to get her back indoors. By the time they reached the side entrance that would lead them to the back elevator, they were both soaked from head to toe. Kennedy laughed like a kid splashing around in a swimming pool during summer break while Malik cursed beneath his breath.

"You are an extremely bad influence on me, Ms. Daniels," Malik fumed.

"Oh, so it's Ms. Daniels again, huh?" Kennedy smirked.

Malik snatched a hand towel from a supply cart that was propped against a wall near the elevator bank. He used a corner of it to wipe the water from Kennedy's forehead. Her eyes were closed and she opened herself to his gentle touch. He wanted to speak, but his heart had expanded until it blocked his vocal chords. He silently stroked her face and hair, mesmerized by the slight smile on her lips and cursing the fact that he was so gone over a woman who he was supposed to be helping to recover.

Chapter 8

Nona Torres, a gorgeous Latina nurse who worked at the facility, had set her sights on Malik shortly after she began working there. Nona wasn't looking for a long-term love affair, marriage or two-point-five kids with Malik. She found him incredibly sexy and a perfect candidate for a few good rolls around in the sack. And that was all she wanted.

As a lowly orderly, Malik did not have the qualifications she was looking for in a life partner. Nona had set her fishing rod dangling in deeper waters to snag one of the doctors or administrators she worked with. Or she might try for the rich clients she served, some of whom were not permanently or overly incapacitated.

No, Nona's interest in Malik was purely physical and she was the type of woman who got anything and everything she wanted sooner or later.

Nona started her seduction of the elusive Malik Crawford with a few innocent comments, a well-placed compliment and random coincidental meetings around the facility. The man who had many of the women there squeezing their thighs together and batting their eyelashes was definitely a hard case to figure. He was polite and courteous, but hardly what could be considered sociable. This made Nona all the more determined and the other staff members were practically taking bets on whether she'd wear him down or not.

Malik was not deaf, dumb or blind, which he'd have to be to miss out on the vibe that Nona was throwing at him. He chuckled to himself, but kept a safe distance. The last thing he needed was to get involved with a coworker, especially one as voluptuous as Nona. Malik could tell that she was trouble from across the room and he had had enough trouble with women to last a lifetime. However, a couple of weeks before Kennedy became a client at Stillwater, when Malik was feeling desperately lonely and dejected, he took Nona up on her offer to go out for a drink. Seated at a table for two at the back of Murphy's, a little jazz spot that offered mellow music and great booze, Nona turned up the heat. After five minutes of conversation, he knew that not only did he not desire to be with her, the hard-on he'd been maintaining all night from the moment she'd arrived at Murphy's wearing a clinging red dress, stilettos and showing enough cleavage to stop traffic, was starting to diminish. He walked her to her car after only two drinks and as she pressed her stacked body up against his, her hot tongue sending electric jolts through his mouth, he fought the urge to take what she was offering him. The driving thought in his brain as he drove home alone was that had he slept with her, ten minutes after climaxing, he'd have wished to be away from her.

For some men, that wouldn't be that big of a deal. They had no problem bedding a woman who they didn't like or even know. In his earlier days, he had been one of those men looking for a good time every chance they got. Now, however, he knew that sex with a woman for whom you didn't have at least a sense of liking, was just sex and would leave him as fulfilled as masturbation did. He was looking for *more*.

Malik let himself fantasize about Kennedy Daniels being *more*. She was everything that he wanted in a mate—smart, independent and sincere. Physically, she was without question the sexiest woman he'd ever laid eyes on. Unlike many women, Nona included, who believed they had to spread their goods for display in order to attract a man, Kennedy was breathtaking in even the most concealing clothing possible. An oversize T-shirt and baggy sweats did nothing to diminish her appeal. Listening to her talk, hearing her laugh and just watching the change of expressions on her beautiful face was a prize for him. Yet Malik did not kid himself. While he allowed fantasies of a relationship with her to enter his brain for a few fleeting moments at a time, he knew that there wasn't a remote possibility that those fantasies would come true.

Women like Kennedy Daniels did not fall in love with men like him and even if they did, there was no way that their lifestyles could coexist. She was from the part of town where his people only ventured to clean up or provide other services. Malik reminded himself of that fact every time he caught his mind lingering on her for too long. He would continue to be her friend while she was a client at Stillwater, helping her along the road of recovery. When she was well, he would say goodbye and wish her good luck. Period. This was the promise he made to himself even as his body language shouted a different story. That story was picked up on by a few members of the staff, including Nona Torres.

"What's up with you, Malik? Haven't seen you around much lately," Nona said one day as he was headed up to Kennedy's room to say good night. It was the end of his shift and he had already changed into his street clothes. He slung his travel bag over his shoulder as he stopped walking. Nona was blocking his path to the elevator bank.

"I've been around," he answered cautiously.

He had seen her number on his cell-phone caller identification at home a few times over the past couple of months, but had never picked up her call. Right after their date, he'd told her that he wasn't interested in dating at present. He'd explained that he just had too much going on. That seemed to have gone in one of Nona's ears and out the other because she'd simply smiled and said, "We'll see about that."

"You've been around? Humph, yeah, I guess I have seen you around a little bit...your clients have been keeping you pretty busy, huh?"

"No, not any more than usual," Malik answered cautiously, wondering what Nona was getting at.

"Hmm, what's up with that rich chick on seven? What's her story?"

"I don't know what you mean," Malik answered.

"I'm saying, no one ever visits her. She's probably one of these rich, black girls who thinks she's too good for regular folks, right?" Nona asked, as she reached out and traced the collar of Malik's polo shirt.

"Look, Nona, I really don't have time to gossip. It's been a long day, and I really need to get going."

"Oh, so you don't have a minute to spend with a friend? That's cold."

"Don't take it like that. I'm just tired, that's all. I'll catch up with you some other time."

"Yeah, all right, Malik, I'm going to hold you to that," she said. "By the way, Malik, the exit's that way," she said, pointing in the opposite direction of where Malik was walking.

He bit his tongue without responding and continued walking. Her insinuations were obvious, and he knew that if she had noticed the amount of time he was spending with Kennedy, so had the others. The last thing he wanted was for people to start gossiping about Kennedy and hinting that anything improper was going on between them.

If there was one thing Malik disliked about his job, it was the way some of his coworkers talked about the clients that came through Stillwater. It was true that many of them were wealthy. A person would have to be in order to afford what Stillwater charged. Most major medical insurances only covered between one-half and three-quarters of the costs and many of their clients underwent rehabilitation for as many as three months. What bothered Malik, however, was the fact that some of the staff held an automatic prejudice against the clients as though they were not real people with real problems. While the clients were treated with respect and irreproachable care, the conversations in the faculty lounges always rolled around to how nasty this client was or what a slut that one was.

Malik never got involved in those conversations and steered clear of the usual suspects who participated in them. He abhorred being judged by external things such as money and occupation himself, so there was no way he would stoop so low as to judge someone else by those same inconsequential measurements. Had he not felt that way, there was no way that he would have taken the time to get to know Kennedy, and Malik truly believed that that would have been his tragic loss.

Chapter 9

On the day that the fiberglass cast and the half a
dozen metal pins that held her shattered kneecap
together while it healed were removed, Kennedy
felt like she was finally getting a piece of her life
back. The smell of skin now uncovered by the cast
was very unpleasant and she shuddered to think
what it looked like. Nurse Crosby felt the need to
fill her in.

"Oh, we're going to have to treat your skin…get
it back to that pretty complexion you've got. Right
now, it's all wrinkled and drawn from the middle of
your thigh, right down to your foot. Looks skinny,
too, but that's just because it was cooped up in that

tight cast for so long. Don't worry, dear, it'll soon be as good as new."

Kennedy's happiness at her newfound freedom from bondage was not in the least dampened by the fact that her muscles had become so stiff that she could barely lift her leg. She knew that it would take time before she could move about freely and quickly, but having the cast off at long last was the first step. As Malik wheeled her for what she hoped would be the last time from the examination room to the physical therapy ward, she was giddy with excitement.

"Don't be trying to go out and run marathons just yet, Kennedy," Malik joked.

"Oh, but I am. You don't know how hard it was being trapped in all that plaster and stuff. I can't wait to get this leg working again," Kennedy replied.

Malik stayed inside during Kennedy's session, although it hurt him to watch the pain and agony that contorted her pretty face as she attempted to stand with her weight on both legs. Sweat broke out on her forehead and stained the material of her sweater under her armpits as she fought to ignore the pain and make strides toward her recovery. He fought the urge to spring from his seat and help her as she clutched the handrails and inched up the walkway. He knew that she had to do it alone, and he had the utmost confidence that she would persevere. All the same, he wanted to help her and shield her from any hurt.

The sudden realization that Kennedy had come to mean a great deal to him scared Malik. He was also afraid that people would begin to notice how devoted he'd become to her. He also worried that she would soon realize the feelings he had for her, as well.

He comforted himself with the thought that soon she would be leaving Stillwater and that would bring an end to what had been brewing between them. He considered that perhaps distancing himself from her sooner was the best course of action. Before he could act, however, he ended up having a heated argument with Jessica Nelson, one of the seventh-floor nurses who just so happened to be a close friend of Nona's. Jessica was part of the gossip mill, and it was nothing for her to drop insinuations about the clients. She crossed the line with Malik one day, however, and he lost it.

"So, Malik, I see you've got yourself a little side hustle these days," Jessica said, cornering him as he filled out a tag to have a wheelchair repaired and stored it in a supply closet near the nurses' station.

"What are you talking about, Jessica?" Malik asked.

"Well, I mean, everybody knows you've been spending a lot of time with Miss Daniels…room seven west? We're just all wondering how much money you've tapped her for. These society chicks that come through here pay well for a certain type of *company,* if you know what I mean."

Malik spun on his heels to face Jessica. The nasty sneer that curled her otherwise attractive face made her look every bit as devilish on the outside as she was inside. Blind fury sent scorching heat from his brain to his toes. He took two large menacing steps toward her and her expression changed in a flash to fear.

"You spiteful bitch…you'd better watch your dirty little mouth. Don't let appearances fool you. You don't know me like that to step in my face talking trash," he growled.

Jessica took a step backward, moving out of the confines of the closet into the well-lit corridor.

"Whoa, you'd better back up, Malik. All I said was—"

"I heard what you said, and I hope you heard me. Watch what comes out of your mouth before you get yourself hurt."

"Hurt? By who? Certainly not by you. I don't appreciate you threatening me, either," Jessica screeched.

"No, baby doll, that wasn't a threat. That was a promise."

"Don't threaten me, Malik."

"And don't you mess with me, Jessica."

"Whatever. I don't know who you think you are, and I damned sure don't know what Nona sees in your tired behind," Jessica said.

It was all Malik could do not to take his hand and wipe the smugness off of her face. Instead, he

clutched his fists against the side of his pants legs
and moved past her, away from the stares of the
people at the nurses' station. He felt Jessica's hateful
eyes boring into his back, but he continued walking
without looking back until he had turned the corner
and was out of sight. His pager vibrated at his side
at precisely that moment and he looked down to
find room number seven west displayed on the
screen. Kennedy.

He toyed with the idea of not responding to her call.
He was too upset, and he didn't want her to see him
in such a sour mood. She didn't deserve to have her
sunny days dampened by vile innuendos. After a
moment or two of contemplation, he realized that her
sweet disposition would be the best medicine for his
current agitation. He made a beeline for Kennedy's
room.

"Are you decent?" Malik asked as he stuck his
head in the doorway after knocking three short raps
on the wood.

"Get in here, you." Kennedy laughed. "Look. I
just got these in the mail," she continued.

Malik stepped farther into the room and joined
Kennedy on the two-seater. He took the package she
held out in front of her.

"Books on tape," he read from the label.

"Yep. I ordered *Brother Odd* and *The Husband*
by Dean Koontz and Stephen King's latest. Isn't
that great?"

"Oh, yeah, it's cool, but I told you that I'd read them all to you," Malik said.

His brows knotted with concern as he suspected that perhaps he had overstayed his welcome with Kennedy. He worried that she might be trying to tell him that she wanted some space. They had discovered a mutual interest in science fiction and mystery novels and Malik had brought in his collection of Dean Koontz thrillers. After Kennedy selected a title that she had never read before, they would sit shoulder to shoulder, Malik reading and Kennedy clutching his wrist during the scary parts.

"I know and you've been great, but I also know that you've got to be getting tired of reading out loud. This way…we can listen together," she said.

Malik's sigh of relief was audible. He spent the rest of that evening seated by Kennedy's side listening to a twisted tale of a man who enlists the help of an antiaddiction group to help him kick his smoking habit, only to find that there's a high price for anyone who strays from the program, including electric shock and body mutilation.

Malik dared to drape his arm around Kennedy's shoulders and when she nestled against him, his heart felt full to bursting. They fell asleep in the middle of chapter four and Malik felt like he had the most peaceful sleep of his life. When he awakened, it was after three o'clock in the morning. He brushed his lips gently against Kennedy's forehead and slid his arm from beneath her. He slipped out of her room, taking the back elevator out of the building to avoid being noticed.

When his supervisor called him into his office the next morning, Malik instinctively knew that it wouldn't be good. His suspicions were confirmed when Dennis Grayson informed him that it had been brought to his attention that Malik had been slacking on his duties of late, due to the extra time and attention he was paying one client in particular. It didn't take a rocket scientist to know who had brought the situation to Grayson's attention, considering the fact that the man rarely came out of his office and could barely put his staff's names and faces together.

Malik didn't attempt to dispute Grayson's allegation. He remained silent while he was reminded of Stillwater's policies and procedures, warned about future infractions and told that he was being reassigned to the fifth-floor clients. The fifth-floor day shift client assistant, Rodney Singh, would take over care for Kennedy and the rest of Malik's seventh-floor clients.

Malik didn't have an opportunity to tell Kennedy himself. She paged him twice during the day, but he waited until his shift had ended and he had signed out for the day before he signed into the building as a visitor and went to see her.

"Malik, I'm so sorry. I didn't mean to cause you

any trouble. Maybe I can talk to your boss and try to smooth things over for you," Kennedy suggested.

"No, no, trust me, it's not even worth it. Just as long as Rodney's taking good care of you," Malik answered.

"Oh, he was fine…doesn't talk much, but he was okay."

Despite the change in Malik's responsibilities, there were no restrictions on his personal time, which he chose to spend with Kennedy. He joined her during his lunch hour out near the lagoon and stopped in to see her every evening before he left for the night. Often a quick good night ended up stretching deliciously into an hour or two that neither of them were willing to tear themselves away from.

It wasn't until Malik had to take a few days off to travel out of town to attend a funeral that Kennedy realized how much she had grown to depend on his company. While she expressed sincere condolences at the loss of his uncle, she felt a nagging sensation of abandonment. Although she'd never share that sentiment with him, she could not stop herself from feeling it.

With perfect timing, Skyy surprised her with a visit two days after Malik left town. Her unexpected arrival was just in time to stave off the loneliness that had begun to scratch at the edges of Kennedy's spirit.

"Girl, you are looking good. Ten times better

than the last time I saw you. Give me some love," Skyy beamed.

"Thank you, thank you. I wish I could say the same, but, you know…" Kennedy joked.

For the first time, the sheer humor in her statement outweighed the bitterness at the source of her remark. For her it was a sign that perhaps she would eventually get used to her loss of sight.

"You don't need to see me to know that I'm looking fabulous, as usual. That's what I do!" Skyy quipped.

Laden with packages, Skyy dropped all kinds of goodies onto Kennedy's bed. They spent the remainder of the day sampling brioche, the sweet pastries Skyy had brought directly from southern Italy that melted in your mouth like cotton candy. They sprayed on designer perfumes from famous Italian industry notables and tried on handmade shirts and sweaters from the rural mountain areas of the North. Skyy's enthusiasm and love for the place she was temporarily calling home was infectious and Kennedy hoped to one day get to see the country in every sense of the word.

Kennedy took Skyy on a tour of the facility and they lingered at what had now become her favorite place—the lagoon.

"I spend a lot of time down here. It's so peaceful," Kennedy informed.

"Yeah, it's really beautiful. Romantic. A woman could get caught up down here, with the right guy.

Shimmering water, fragrant flowers…you'd better watch out or one of these old geezers who just got a new hip might try to put the moves on you," Skyy joked. "And, since I happen to know that you have been out of circulation for a minute, you just might be open to hooking up with a geriatric Jack."

Kennedy didn't respond, her thoughts having wandered away to Malik. She wondered what he was doing and if he'd missed their midday meal by the water as much as she had that day.

"Okay, if I'd wanted to be ignored, I would have gone to visit my folks. What's up with you?"

"Huh? I'm sorry. I was just thinking," Kennedy said.

"Yeah, that much is obvious. What's up with that big Kool-Aid grin on your face? What are you *just thinking* about? Or should I ask *who?*"

"Nothing…I mean, nobody. Just a friend." Kennedy blushed.

"Spill," Skyy commanded, dropping down to the grass and pulling Kennedy down beside her.

She stretched her legs out front of her, leaned back on the palms of her hands and waited.

"Really, Skyy, he's just a friend. He's…he was one of the client assistants who was assigned to me, but they switched him to another floor a couple of days ago. Anyway, he's just been really nice to me since I've been here…you know, taking really good care of me. He's a nice guy."

Skyy eyed her friend's expressionless look with skepticism.

"Uh huh, so what are you leaving out?"

"What? Nothing, I swear. He's a nice guy and, you know, it's pretty boring here and he helps me pass the time. That's all there is to it."

Kennedy's last statement was adamant, but Skyy was far from being convinced. She knew that there had to be a reason why Kennedy was being evasive about a potential relationship, although she had no idea what that reason could be. She waited until later in the evening before broaching the subject again.

"How about I wash your hair for you? I've got some homemade shampoo that's to die for. This little old Sicilian woman named Rosalia mixes the stuff in her kitchen and sells it out of empty baby food jars. Come on."

While Skyy lathered Kennedy's hair and massaged her scalp under the warm water, Kennedy relaxed and inhaled the deliciously fruity fragrance. Lost in thoughts that transported her mind to another time and another place, she felt a heady anticipation inside. She knew that feeling only came from one source and despite how hard she tried to deny it, that source was love.

"So, when do I get to meet this *nice guy* who's *nobody?*" Skyy asked as she toweled Kennedy's hair dry.

Kennedy smiled, knowing that she had been even

less successful at fooling Skyy than she had been at misleading herself.

"He's out of town…at a funeral."

"Too bad. Well, maybe next time. I've got to go spend some time with the folks down in North Cakallaky. My dad's prostate is acting up again and you know my mom isn't good in crises."

"Oh, no, Skyy. Why didn't you tell me that sooner?"

"Aah, you know I hate to be the bearer of bad news. Hopefully, it's nothing too serious. His doctor is running some more tests. I'm going to spend a few weeks with them, running errands and taking him back and forth to his doctor's visits. But, my dear, I'll definitely head back up here to see you before I fly out to Italy again. In the meantime, behave yourself."

"Me? Of course, don't I always behave?" Kennedy asked devilishly.

Skyy left Kennedy in a state of serious introspection. There was no sense to be made out of her feelings for Malik—a guy who she'd known for just a few short weeks but felt like she'd known for a lifetime just the same.

She knew that she and Malik had no business being together. The circumstances under which they met were just the tip of the iceberg. There was no way that Malik would be acceptable to her parents. The Daniels had made it clear that their daughters were to choose men whose backgrounds mirrored their own.

Kennedy's privileged upbringing was one in which she was taught that there are two types of black people—the right ones and the wrong ones. The right kind of black people hold Ivy League degrees from the likes of Harvard or Yale or, in the alternative, from historically black institutions such as Spelman or Morehouse. The right kind of black people wore with pride their skin tones, and those ranging from a shade lighter than eggshell to that of a shiny new copper penny were held in higher esteem. The right kind of black people know which fork is the salad fork, summer in Paris and belong to Jack and Jill of America, Inc.

Kennedy had been taught early that there were undeniably the wrong kind of black folks—those who hold mundane nine-to-five clerical jobs or spend any portion of their lives on public assistance. The wrong kind of black folks don't know the difference between a Merlot and a Cabernet and spend a week, if they are lucky, at the Jersey Shore each summer.

All of her life, Kennedy and Madison were admonished to stay away from the wrong kind of black folks. Up until the fateful night of her car accident, it appeared as though Kennedy would continue down the path her parents had laid out for her. Shattered glass and the crunch of metal, however, had sent her in another direction—one in which a blue-collar man from a working-class background had captured her heart.

Chapter 10

Malik walked around the spacious living room of Kennedy's apartment, studying the various framed photographs. He picked out Madison, Kennedy's sister, immediately in a picture of the two of them posed next to a huge Christmas tree. Kennedy appeared to be a few years younger than she was now and Madison was a younger, slightly fairer in complexion, version of her. He viewed the photographs of her parents, of the four of them together and a couple of shots of Kennedy alone. All of the pictures had been posed in luxuriant surroundings. If he had had any doubts that the Daniels family was well-to-do, these pictures erased them.

Various educational degrees—undergraduate from Princeton and a masters and PhD from George-town University—hung from the walls. Malik was impressed yet again by Kennedy's achievements. He was even more impressed, however, by the fact that despite her background and her pedigree, Kennedy remained unpretentious and as down-to-earth as a woman in her circumstances was allowed.

Malik had been waiting in front of her condo when the Stillwater transport van brought her and her new friend—a two-year-old Seeing Eye dog, Muppet—home. Muppet and Kennedy had been in-troduced toward the end of the rehabilitation process at Stillwater. The focus of what they termed vision loss adjustment therapy at Stillwater was first placed on developing Kennedy's sense of independence and confidence at living with her limitations. Muppet had already received his training through a program that rears and prepares dogs for guide work.

Once they were placed together, Kennedy's job was to reinforce what Muppet already knew and add new skills that applied to her life. Some of the common things people trained their Seeing Eye dogs to assist them with were things such as finding a place to sit, locating the push button at cross-walks, or recognizing a particular person by name. By the time Muppet and Kennedy were put togeth-er, Kennedy had established a poise that allowed her to learn to handle Muppet without angst.

Within a few days, the pair were like old friends and Kennedy, who'd never owned a dog of her own, could be found on the floor of her room at Stillwater snuggling with Muppet, who lapped up the attention greedily. Kennedy was already amazed by how much Muppet knew how to do on his own and slowly she began to trust his eyes and senses as much as she had once upon a time trusted her own.

Kennedy had shyly given Malik the address and the keys the night before and he'd promised, with equal nervousness, to be there to help her get settled. As her recovery at Stillwater had progressed and her release date drew near, she had thought that she could handle things on her own. However, as she made the final preparations for her return to her home, her initial thoughts gave way to doubt.

The assisted-living specialist, Martha Duncan, had been cautioning her that resuming her life would be tough and that not having at least a little bit of help would make it even more difficult.

As Skyy was back in Italy and Kennedy was reluctant to ask her to put her work and life on hold to babysit her, she considered asking her mother to come. For a split second she considered having her mother living in her apartment with her and just as quickly as the thought had entered her mind, she dismissed it. Although Elmira always meant well, it wouldn't take long before she'd shredded Kennedy's last nerve. Besides, she later found out that her contemplation was wasted because her mother had accompanied her father on a trip to Mannheim, Germany, for a medical symposium. He was serving as a guest on an international panel of surgical specialists.

When Kennedy decided to ask Malik to help her transition from Stillwater to her home, it was with an equal amount of confidence that he was the best choice and trepidation that he would accept. She could not entirely dismiss the thought that perhaps she had overworked his kind nature and asking him to help her outside of the confines of his job was asking too much. She was relieved when he accepted without hesitation and he was relieved that she could not see the euphoric grin that covered his face at her request.

He'd arrived early and surveyed the apartment, taking it upon himself to move a few pieces of furniture around that he thought would impede her movement.

"It feels so good to finally be home," Kennedy exclaimed as she stood in the middle of her kitchen.

"I hear you. You've got a beautiful place," Malik complimented. "So what would you like to do first?"

Malik guided Kennedy to the sofa. Once seated Kennedy leaned back, relaxing for the first time that day.

"I was so nervous about coming home, but I just realized something," she said.

"What's that?" Malik said, stroking the top of Muppet's head.

"This is my home. I decorated it and organized it. I know exactly where everything is, so why should I be anxious about making my way around it?"

"You shouldn't be. Although I do have a confession," Malik said, hesitating. "I moved a few things around while I waited for you…just to make it easier for you to get around. You're not going to hit me, are you?"

"That depends, Mr. Crawford. What'd you move?"

Malik explained how he opened up the living room a bit, moving the sofa from it's place in front of the window to a more advantageous location against the wall. That way, her path to the windows and to the room that served as her office was clear. He also moved the two plant stands to the corners of the room. She did not object as he led her around the room, counting steps between various spots and learning landmarks that she could use to get around without tripping.

Together they organized the kitchen, placing Braille labels on canned goods and dividing the shelves in the cabinet by putting canned fruit on one side of a shelf, canned veggies on another and all the same kind of boxed foods together on another shelf. The baking stuff was grouped together on one shelf and everything was labeled.

They went grocery shopping for fresh fruits, veg-
etables and meats. Most of the refrigerated items
were identifiable by the shape of the container. For
things like salad dressings and other condiments,
whose bottles are all very similar, they used Braille
labels. The first few days were rocky as Kennedy
dealt with anger over the things she could not do on
her own. She was embarrassed at times by having
to ask Malik if a shirt matched with a certain pair
of pants or if she'd put on the right color lipstick.
His patience with her irritation helped those feelings
to pass, and the more comfortable she grew in
asking for help, the easier things became for her.
She also grew more independent with each passing
day, yet for the things she did need help with, Malik
was right there.

Chapter 11

Kennedy stood in the entryway of the darkened living room. She listened intently, until the rhythm of Malik's breathing reached her ears. He was standing near the window and to her trembling legs the distance seemed a thousand miles away. She walked slowly across the living room, one hand stretched in front of her. She counted the steps in her head, estimating her way to the sofa, past the plant stand and finally to Malik. She reached out, her fingers tentatively making contact with the soft cotton fabric of the top of his pajama pants. She moved her hand slowly up the length of his naked back. The smoothness of his skin beneath her fingers triggered a clenching sensation in the center of her belly. She let her fingers be her eyes as they traveled the path of his torso.

Malik did not move. He had been waiting in the stillness of that night and countless nights before—even before he had met her. It was as if all of the women in his life before Kennedy had just been fillers. Not one of them had ever touched that part of his soul that needed to be touched and loved. Kennedy was the woman he'd been dreaming about before he was even aware that something was missing in his life. From the moment he'd first talked to her, even during her suffering and pain, his heart had finally felt complete. He'd wanted to hold her from that first day and love her past her pain. Without realizing it at the time, he had done just that and she had done so much more for him.

Every morning he'd wake up on the sofa in Kennedy's living room, feeling restless. He'd get up and make a fresh pot of coffee. Despite Kennedy's protests he'd also make a pot of hot cereal, usually oatmeal, her favorite, and slice a few pieces of melon for her breakfast.

"I can learn how to do this for myself, Malik," she'd say.

"I know you can but I want to do it," he'd reply.

And she'd let him every morning. He'd feed Muppet and take the dog for a walk before heading off to work at Stillwater. The days passed slowly for him as his thoughts traveled back to Kennedy. He called on each of his breaks to check on her and each time she would chide him for being overprotective. Secretly, however, she reveled in his attention. When he returned to the apartment in the evenings, slightly apprehensive about entering using the key she'd given him, she'd be happy to see him, erasing his doubts. Together, they'd prepare an evening meal, clean up in the kitchen and go through Kennedy's mail.

He helped her write out checks for bills and answer the never-ending correspondence from friends and associates wishing her well. Finally, as the night fell around them, they would settle on the sofa and either read from one of their mystery novels or listen to music and talk.

Their routine had become commonplace to them without any fanfare or heavy contemplation on either of their parts. When Kennedy would retire to her bedroom for the night, Malik remained in the living room, but his thoughts climbed into bed with Kennedy and wrapped themselves around her. For the first couple of nights he had tried to settle himself in the guest bedroom, but was unable to get comfortable. He felt as though he were too far away from her. Being on the living room sofa seemed to put him more at ease. Just as he strove to protect and shelter her during her waking hours, he wanted to hold her in his arms and listen to her breathing at night. He settled for being close enough to hear her if she cried out for help. Then he would spring into action, ready to serve her, body and soul.

Even so, the past few days spent sleeping on her sofa had been torture for him. But he would not allow himself to push her. For the longest time he had viewed their relationship as caregiver and patient. Then they'd moved to a stage of mutual friendship and respect. Yet he'd felt the shift once again when they'd moved toward love and lust, and although he'd fought it intellectually, his heart could not deny what he felt for her. He wanted Kennedy as a friend and a lover. However, he told himself that if their relationship moved beyond friendship, it would be on her terms and at her discretion. As much as it tormented him being so near to her and not being able to be with her, he waited.

Ironically, he had been wanting her to touch him like this for so long that now that the moment was here, he felt paralyzed. As her hands glided up his back, his heart seized in uncontrollable spasms. Every muscle in his body ached to be visited by the softness of her, yet part of him now resisted. As strong and independent as she was, Malik had spied the vulnerable part of her that she kept hidden. The passion that had been building between them for the past few weeks could not be denied, but he did not want to do anything that would cause her one moment of pain. The question that burned continuously in his brain was what he could possibly do for a woman like Kennedy and, as yet, no answer had become clear to him, no matter how long he thought about it.

Right now, however, his mind would not allow him to think clearly. Kennedy had moved closer, her body pressing against his back. He could feel the voluptuous mass of her breasts on his shoulder blades. She ran her hands around the front of his body slowly, across his ribs and his stomach muscles contracted at her touch.

"Malik," she whispered, her lips brushing against his shoulder.

"Kennedy...I," he began, but lust caused his throat to close around the rest of his words.

"Ssh, I know, I know," Kennedy said.

Malik knew that she did, in fact, know what was in his heart and mind, just as he knew what was in hers. It did not matter that they were from two very different backgrounds, had grown up worlds apart and now lived lifestyles that were as far removed as different universes. Theirs were kindred spirits, meant to find each other at this time for reasons that were outside of either of their abilities to grasp.

Malik turned to face her. In the darkness her smooth skin glistened. He moved his hand up the nape of her neck into the silky brown hair that hung down her back. He wanted to lose himself inside of her, to find a place where doubt and worry did not exist. Malik knew that within her he could find the peace that his spirit craved. Slowly and deliberately, he bent his head down towards hers and covered her mouth with his. She sighed when their tongues touched and began to dance a slow wet dance, as if she, too, had been waiting since forever for their music to begin. Their first kiss, after breathless weeks of feeling the magnetic pull between them, was sweet as chocolate—more satisfying than either thought possible.

Malik's arms closed around Kennedy's taut body, pulling her so close that his desire for her could no longer be disguised. His breathing became erratic as visions of her body ricocheted around his brain. He'd seen her sad, he'd seen her smiling and happy. He'd seen her scared and wiped tears of frustration from her beautiful face. All of those images had pulled him to her, allowing him to get to know her better than any words ever could.

Malik pulled himself away from her reluctantly. He scooped her effortlessly up off of her feet and into his arms. Her lips found his again in the darkness as he carried her across the living room, down the hallway and into her bedroom.

"Is there another light switch?" he asked huskily, aware of only the bright track lighting that lined the ceiling in her bedroom.

"There, above the bed," she said, pointing.

Malik lay Kennedy down on the bed and turned

on the soft lamp above the headboard. The room was bathed in gentle, dim light.

"I want to see you," he said.

Kennedy reached up, running her fingers down the side of his face.

"I do see you," she responded.

Malik lay beside her, studying her body with wonder. The white gown she wore was made of formfitting fabric, with thin straps trimmed in lace. It hugged her breasts and stopped in the middle of her thighs. He traced her collarbone with his fingers first, and then his tongue took their place. As large as his hands were, one of them was not enough to cover the fullness of her breast, although he tried his best. He squeezed and molded the flesh and then, with two fingers, concentrated on the nipples, which were pointed and erect. He tugged at the top of her gown until one mound was freed and then the other. Nipples as dark as milk chocolate stood proudly, beckoning him it seemed.

When Malik's warm tongue circled one of her nipples, Kennedy's back arched. The sensation was almost more than she could bare. He closed his mouth over her, sucking all of her chocolate as if his very life depended on it. He alternated between breasts, giving them an equal amount of attention and concentrating on them both in their entirety.

Kennedy began to feel feverish as the passion building within her multiplied. Her hands played with the back of Malik's head and neck. She loved the way the coarseness of his thick hair felt against her chin and in her hands. His scent—a combination of masculinity and soap—filled her senses to the brim and as it mingled with the smell of their sex together, she felt as if she were so full that she would explode.

"I'll be right back," Malik said, after finally being able to pull himself away from her tasty Hershey's kisses.

He went into the living room where his clothing was folded in a pile near the sofa. From his pants pocket, he retrieved the package of condoms that he'd bought earlier in the week. When he'd made the purchase, he'd felt somewhat guilty, as if he were scheming on making a move on Kennedy. Now, he realized that it had not been him who had been scheming at all. It had been fate guiding and planning the course of their relationship to bring them to this point, this night. He was now ecstatic that a lack of preparation would not interrupt their destiny.

When he returned to the room, Kennedy had removed her gown and was sitting nude on the side of the bed. He walked over to her, stopping in front of her. With his left hand, he stroked her hair and the side of her face. To him she seemed even more beautiful than when he'd left her moments ago, and he didn't doubt that every time from that moment on that he looked at her, her beauty would have multiplied. She was delicate and at the same time tenacious. She was soft, yet strong. She had endured so much and still she was fresh and new. Malik felt in his marrow that he would never meet another woman like Kennedy. His only desire at that moment was to plant himself inside of her and stake his claim. For as long as was possible, she would be his.

Kennedy reached both hands around his waist and pulled both Malik's pajama bottoms and his boxers down to his knees at the same time. Malik stepped out of them, kicking them behind him with his feet. Kennedy ran her hands up and down his thighs, envisioning the tight muscular limbs in her mind. She already knew that he was strong from the way he'd lifted and carried her about at Stillwater. She could tell that his body was fit and well toned, her fingers having yet to meet a flabby spot on him. The width of his lips was evident as they devoured her mouth and breasts. Her fingers had played with the bushy hair of his eyebrows and the curly lashes on his lids. In her mind she'd used what her hands had told her about him to create a visual of the man who stood in front of her and that image was breathtaking.

She reached out, taking his now fully erect penis in her hands. It pulsed against her palm. She tightened her grip, encircling him in warmth. Malik tore open one of the condom wrappers, removing the latex. He placed it on the tip of his penis and Kennedy took over, rolling the plastic down his shaft with deliberately slow motions. When it was in place, she held on to him, massaging him with tender strokes. Finally, she slid backwards on the bed and Malik followed. His mouth found hers again, covering her with kisses so sweet that she melted. A river flowed between her legs and when his hand slid between her satiny thighs, all he found was wetness and warmth as she parted her legs for him.

"You're so ready," he whispered into her mouth.

"Just for you," she breathed.

Kennedy raised her legs, planting both feet on the mattress beneath her as Malik positioned himself above her. As he inserted himself into her waiting nest, she gasped. He froze, unwilling to cause her one instant of discomfort. It was Kennedy who held on to his hips and guided him inside of her, pulling until their bodies met, pelvis to pelvis.

"Okay?" he asked timidly.

"Mmm, hmm," Kennedy moaned, her face contorted with pleasure.

Her hips arched against his, signaling him that she was, indeed, ready for him. He began to move, matching her rolling hips move for move. Their sweat mingled as their bodies moved into and against one another. Everything that Malik had dreamed about in this moment paled in comparison to the reality of it. He had not doubted her ability to satisfy him. What caught him completely off guard was how much making love to her would gratify every part of him, mind, body and soul.

Chapter 12

"You know, I never told anyone this, but the night of the accident…I think I died."

"What? You mean you passed out, right?"

"No, I mean…I know it sounds crazy, but I really think I passed away. Only, there was no bright, white light like you hear in the movies. There was this moment, right before the car hit the pole when everything seemed to stand still for just a split second and it was like, I knew that it was over. Then I guess the car hit the pole and that was it. Later, when I was in the hospital, I started seeing images of myself in the smashed car, and I could see myself slumped over in the seat, bleeding and not moving. I saw it all. At first I thought it was a dream, just my imagination working overtime because of the drugs."

"But now you think it was more than that?"

"Yes, I do. I think I was actually outside of my body looking at the accident. I'm talking about before the paramedics and the police arrived, when it was just me in the mangled car beneath the driving rain. Sounds crazy, right?"

Malik shifted so that his body was even closer to Kennedy, his arms tight around her torso.

"I don't think it's crazy, but I will tell you this, I think I'm going to send those emergency response guys a big box of chocolate tomorrow."

"For what?" Kennedy giggled.

"For saving you...for me," Malik said.

He reached down and placed his finger beneath Kennedy's chin. In the soft light her hazel eyes stared straight ahead as Malik gazed into them. Over the past couple of weeks since she'd been back at home, she'd stopped hiding her eyes from him behind sunglasses as she did around other people. That simple act spoke of the level of trust and openness she felt toward him. To look into her wide and unseeing eyes, but knowing all along that she saw him better than most people he'd known who had twenty-twenty vision, reaffirmed Malik's belief that she'd come into his life at the right time and for a reason. He knew that she could only see fuzzy outlines of figures, but he hoped that his words showed her the depth of his feelings for her.

Kennedy smiled. She moved closer to Malik, wanting to be as close to him as was physically possible. Beneath his wings is where she felt like anything was possible and like nothing could go wrong. She knew that she was just pretending. She wasn't naive enough to believe that Malik had the power to shelter her from all of life's storms. She'd learned the hard way that it did not matter where a person came from, how much money or prestige one's family had, every human being was made of flesh and bone that could be torn or broken. For a little while, however, she pretended that what they had was invincible.

It had been a night of arduous lovemaking. Their first time together stretched into hours and then the next day and still they lingered in one another's arms. The sun rose, bringing a new day and with it came a renewed lust for each other that could not be satiated, no matter how hard they tried. They answered the physical demands on their bodies for nourishment, snacking on whatever they could find in the kitchen that didn't require much preparation. They slept when fatigue overtook them, touched and explored whenever curiosity struck them and talked as often as words found their way to the surface of their lips.

"Your childhood sounds like you had so much

fun. I can't imagine hanging out like you did… going to parties and stuff like that. When I was a kid, everything I did…every party, every activity was supervised and approved by either my parents or someone else's parents. To have the kind of freedom you had must have been a powerful feeling," Kennedy said as she played with the soft bed of hairs on Malik's chest.

"Well, you know what they say about freedom. Sometimes when you have too much of it, it corrupts."

"What do you mean when you say that it *corrupts?*"

"I just mean that sometimes, rules and supervision can be a good thing. Most of the cats I grew up with didn't have a daddy at home to keep them straight and even those of us who did were knuckleheads who didn't always listen. Hanging out in the streets until all hours of the night, fighting and partying…those were some of the best times I ever had and some of the worse," Malik reminisced.

"Yeah, but at least you had them. Sometimes I can't help but feel like I missed out on so much. I feel like I still am missing out. It's like living in a world, but not really feeling like you're part of it. There are so many things that I don't know anything about. I've never had to struggle for anything. I don't know what I'd do if I had to."

"That's not true. Look what you've just made it through. No amount of money or Daddy's connections could change your accident or what happened afterward. It was you, with your will and determination, that brought you out of that accident on top. If that's not struggling, I don't know what is."

"Yeah, but Malik, think about it. If I didn't have a good job, with medical benefits and a family with money, I might not have gotten the quality of care that I received at the hospital. That is what saved my life. My parents paid what the insurance didn't cover for my time at Stillwater. Think about people who don't have access to that level of health care?"

"Yeah, like the people I grew up with. We had the free clinic, which was understaffed and overused, and a box of Band-Aids to keep us going." Malik laughed.

There was no bitterness in his laugh because he had long ago reconciled himself to the fact that in the world there would always be the haves and the have-nots. While he was determined to always be an independent, self-sufficient man who did not have to rely on charity to live, he did not believe that he would ever reach the material success of people like the Daniels. He was okay with that fact and unlike Kennedy, he did not feel bad about it.

"See, that's what I'm talking about. You can laugh about not having a lot of money and stuff, but I think about people like my parents, like me, and I wonder if we'd be able to laugh if suddenly it was all taken away from us. I doubt it seriously."

"Well, I don't know your parents, Kennedy, but

I definitely think you could adjust to anything. You are more than the money and the possessions."

"You think you know me so well, don't you?" Kennedy said, her lips now tasting Malik's skin, still damp from their shower.

"I think I do," Malik answered.

He didn't tell her how much he did know about her, exactly the depth to which he'd been able to peer into her soul in the short time they'd been together. He didn't have to tell her because his touch and his loving showed her.

Chapter 13

"I wish you could come with me," Kennedy said as they stood outside of the security checkpoint.

Her flight would be called to board in just under thirty minutes, giving them scarce enough time to say goodbye.

"Me, too, but from what you've told me, your parents have enough to deal with concerning your sister. We don't need to add meeting some new guy to their plate right now."

"I know," Kennedy agreed.

She had regretted this trip from the moment she'd booked her flight the day before. Actually, she'd regretted it from the second her mother had called.

She'd been frantic. This time Madison's antics had reached an all-time high level of distastefulness, causing embarrassment from which Elmira didn't seem likely to recover anytime soon. Kennedy didn't know what her parents expected her to say or do to her sister, but she could not stay away, especially when she heard the tremor in her mother's voice over the phone.

Elmira was not one to worry. She had always believed that she and she alone controlled her fate and her family's destiny. Kennedy's accident had been just about the worst thing that had ever happened to them. It had shaken Elmira to the core and it seemed that her worrisome youngest child was following up in an effort to demolish what remained of her haughty confidence.

Malik kissed her lips, wishing in that moment that they were alone. He'd spent every night in bed with her since the first night they'd made love, fallen asleep with her in his arms and he doubted seriously he'd get a moment's rest without her gentle snoring against his neck.

The flight to Raleigh-Durham Airport in North Carolina was short and uneventful. Kennedy spent the entire time steeling herself to deal with her parents and her sister. She already knew how the weekend would play out. Her parents would nag, Madison would yell and Kennedy would play the peacemaker. Each of their roles had been defined a long time ago and they played them to perfection.

But this time Madison had crossed the line. According to her mother, Madison's latest exploits had made the front cover of the gossip rags. Madison had been discovered leaving a second-class hotel with Edward Worthington, one of the biggest technology moguls in the country. At fifty-five years old, Worthington was a public figure who had a hand in the political climate of the state of North Carolina and the federal government. His business had a net worth of over five billion dollars. The Daniels and the Worthingtons traveled in the same circles—charity functions, political engagements and more of the same. They would not be considered friends but peers, and as members of the black bourgeoisie, they shared a network of common friends and associates, making it all terribly sordid and embarrassing.

Worthington's wife was a socialite who'd long suspected him of cheating. The media reported that she'd hired a private investigator to confirm her suspicions once and for all in preparation for a gruesome divorce in which she planned to ravage him financially. Photos of Madison and Worthington in a compromising position as the pair left an out-of-the-way hotel was just the kind of dirt she needed to dig his grave, beat him unconscious and then bury him. When the news hit, the confrontation between their parents and Madison was explosive and Madison had stormed out of the house. Two days later when she resurfaced, she was wearing the same clothing and was inebriated beyond belief.

When Kennedy arrived at her parents' home, it was uncomfortably quiet. Madison was in her bedroom, where she'd been holed up for much of the past twenty-four hours since she'd returned. Annemarie, the woman who'd cooked and cleaned for the Daniels since the girls were in grade school, had gotten Madison to eat a couple of light meals and had even cajoled her into taking a hot bath. Other than that, no one had had any interaction with Madison at all.

Kennedy went to her sister's room after having a brief conversation with parents. Elmira was breathing fire over the whole unseemly affair, while Joseph simply sounded drained, as if he was worn out from all the years of Madison's soap opera-worthy escapades and Elmira's dramatic responses. Perhaps it was more than that, but Kennedy had the distinct impression that her father had had more than his spirit could take.

"Maddie?" Kennedy called softly as she tapped on the door.

Muppet stood by her side, looking up at her quizzically. It was the first time Muppet had visited the expansive house and he was still trying to get used to the new surroundings.

The Daniels home had at one time been a plantation. They'd discovered that Joseph's great, great, great grandfather had been a slave on the plantation, owned by a man named Holmes Taggard. It seemed that by the time of the emancipation of the slaves, Taggard had racked up so much gambling debt that he'd already sold off much of his property in pieces. All that remained was the house and about two acres of land surrounding the structure. When Joseph and Elmira first laid eyes on the house early in their marriage, after having discovered its significance in Joseph's family history, the decision to purchase it was a mere formality. They spent nearly a half a million dollars restoring it and told the story of its legacy with pride.

The long corridors of hardwood floors and high ceilings had poor Muppet confused and anxious. Kennedy could relate to the dog's tension, often finding herself longing for the close quarters she now called home in D.C. every time she came here. Her room had remained untouched, as if she was still an eighteen-year-old just heading off for a semester at college.

"Don't worry, Muppet," she soothed the dog, "we'll be back home soon enough."

The even-keeled guide dog stayed by Kennedy's side throughout their visit, going wherever she went as if that was the way things had always been.

"Yes," Madison answered.

Kennedy opened the door and stepped into the room. It smelled of jasmine and clovers, the scents escaping from the aromatherapy candles that were lit and placed around the room.

"Kennedy, what are you doing here?" Madison asked, jumping up from the bed where she'd been lying.

She crossed the wide expanse to the door, putting her arms around her sister when she reached her. She kissed her cheek.

"Don't tell me Mother made you come all the way down here over this mess with me?"

"She didn't make me, but you know her. She's upset and Dad's upset, too. Neither one of them is saying anything that is rational or makes much sense. I wanted to see for myself how you were doing."

Madison sighed, stepping away from her sister.

"Hey, who's your little friend?"

"This is Muppet. Muppet, meet Madison. Muppet is the best eyes a girl could ask for, aren't you, boy?" Kennedy stroked the top of Muppet's head.

"Is he friendly?" Madison asked as she crouched down slowly in front of the dog.

"Very. He's a sweetie pie, right, big boy?"

"Hi there, Muppet. You are a cutie, aren't you?" Madison said, scratching the sensitive place beneath Muppet's jaw.

Muppet responded by licking Madison's chin, prompting a giggle from her.

"He reminds me of the dog Mr. Johnson used to have, remember him?"

"Mr. Johnson, the church janitor? Oh, yeah… Boscoe, right? He was a mutt, though, wasn't he?"

"Yeah, but he was almost the same color as Muppet and the same size."

"They told me he's white and gray…mostly gray, though, with a little beige mixed in."

Madison looked up at her sister, the realization that Kennedy couldn't see kicking in again. Kennedy's face, as beautiful as ever, wore a slight smile. Her eyes were shaded by a slight pair of designer sunglasses, tortoise shell and catlike, giving her an elegant look.

"How are you making out, Kennedy?" Madison asked.

She stood and touched her sister's arm.

"Me? I'm good. I'm really, really good. It's amazing what losing your eyesight can do for you," she joked.

"Kennedy, that's not funny."

"Relax, Maddie, it's okay."

Kennedy moved farther into the room. Madison held her arm, guiding her over to the queen-size, four-poster bed.

"Here, sit."

"So really, Kennedy, tell me how you're making out…the truth. I mean, it's got to be a trip and you're down there in D.C. all by yourself. I was planning to visit and spend some time with you, but Dad said you wanted to be alone."

"I'm not all by myself. I've got Muppet, here, to take care of me."

"Kennedy—"

"Seriously, Madison, I'm doing fine. These past few weeks have been almost mind-blowing, you know. I'm learning new things every day, about myself and the world. I'm forced to pay attention to things now that I'd never taken the time to even notice much less think about. Do I wish I'd never had the accident? Of course, but that doesn't mean that I'm sitting around licking my wounds and crying myself to sleep."

"Of course you're not," Madison said, holding her sister's hand in hers. "You are so strong. Sometimes I wish I could just have half of your strength. Hell, I'd even take an ounce."

"You do, Maddie. You just don't know it."

"No, I don't."

Madison shook her head slowly, a sardonic smile on her lips.

"Maddie…what's going on with you? Come on, talk to me."

"Aah." Madison sighed. "I don't want to talk about it anymore."

"Yeah, I got that from Mother, but, Maddie, you've got to deal with it. It's not going to just go away, you know. What were you thinking? I mean, are you in love with this guy?"

"Come on, Kennedy. You've got to be joking. No, I don't love Eddie Worthington. It was just one of those things that happened. I met him a few months ago at a bar in Charlotte. I knew who he was right away. He bought me a few drinks, we flirted and before I knew it, we were hooking up a couple of times a week. The sex was good and he is a generous and considerate man. I mean, I like men with power and money. There's something about the way he carries himself. I find him extremely attractive."

"But, Madison, he's a married man. An older and very married man."

"I know that, Kennedy, but the way I look at it is this. That's his situation to deal with, not mine."

Madison stood up, moving away from the bed and her sister. She stopped at her dressing table, picking up the soft-bristled brush from the glass tray and began brushing her matted shoulder-length hair. It had grown in since the last time Kennedy had been able to see it.

"My hair is almost as long as yours again, Kennedy. I'm think about cutting it all off again…maybe getting a Mohawk or something. That'd really trip Mother out!"

Madison turned around and faced Kennedy's sour expression.

"Come on, sis, stop acting like what I've done is some sort of crime. Married men fool around on their wives all the time. It wasn't any type of love thing…we were just having a good time. Now it's over and he's at home with his wife, where there was no risk of him ever leaving, anyway, I might add. And his wife's not going anywhere, either, for that matter. All's well that ends well."

"Maddie, you don't mean that."

"I most certainly do. Look, I like men. I meet a man and if something about him strikes me, I go for it. I like to have fun, and I like men with whom I can have a good time with. Jeez, I don't know why everyone is making such a big deal about this. Trust me, despite what Mother thinks, it'll blow over," she said, tossing the hairbrush down.

"Blow over? Madison, this is not some minor slipup. This is major and it's not going to just blow over. Your name has been smeared all over the press."

"Kennedy, you're exaggerating. Daddy ain't exactly Lionel Richie and I damned sure ain't Nicole! By next week the media will have moved on to the next story and I'll be all but forgotten."

Kennedy held her tongue for a moment, trying to control her growing annoyance at her sister's matter-of-fact attitude.

"In the meantime, what about Mother? She is absolutely beside herself," Kennedy said.

"She's always beside herself over one thing or another."

"She worries about you, Madison. We all do. The way you're going, the way you're living your life is not good for you. What is it that you're trying to prove, huh?"

Kennedy rose and slowly made her way to her sister's side. She reached out clumsily until her arm found its way around Madison's shoulder.

For a brief moment, as Madison let herself be hugged by Kennedy, it appeared as though her icy shell was going to melt and she was going to allow her true feelings to be seen. However, that moment was fleeting. It didn't matter what Kennedy said to Madison, there was no penetrating the tough-girl exterior her sister had perfected.

It hurt Kennedy's heart to see her sister trying so hard to be tough and carefree, but it was obvious that Madison was in too much turmoil to even see what she was doing to herself.

Kennedy spent the next few days hanging around the house. She spent most of her time with Madison, holed up in her bedroom in an effort to avoid dealing with Elmira. They listened to music and reminisced about old times, waiting for the storm to pass. They didn't venture out much, especially after the day they were accosted in the bakery by a reporter who recognized Madison. By Friday, the situation seemed to have died down. At least Madison and Elmira were being civil to one another again.

Madison was contemplating going to spend some time alone at the family vacation home in South Florida, but Elmira was reluctant to have her out of her sight. Kennedy took an early morning flight back to D.C. on Saturday morning, the tension of dealing with her family's problems traveling with her. However, as soon as she stepped off the plane and found Malik waiting for her, the worry immediately seeped from her pores. His strong arm around her shoulder, guiding her home, was as effective as it was comforting.

Chapter 14

"**I** can't believe you have me out here in the middle of nowhere. Girl, I'm really going to have to stop messing around with you before I end up getting eaten by a bear or something," Malik said, tossing another log into the fireplace.

Kennedy had rented a cabin situated on the shoreline of the beautiful Shenandoah River. The privately-owned campgrounds were located sixty miles to west of the D.C. metro area. To reach the rustic cabin they traveled on a secluded road, sur-rounded by towering spruce trees and bordered on one side by the river. Their nearest neighbor was a fifteen-minute brisk hike away. The cabin belonged to a colleague of hers at Morgan Stanley, Ben Dailey. Dailey rarely used the cabin for himself, rather he used it as more of an investment property. He rented it out for weekends, and in some cases, for the entire summer season. Kennedy had been there once before when she and Skyy had thrown a bachelorette weekend blast for a mutual friend, Deidre Thompson, before her wedding.

As a child, Kennedy had loved the outdoors, especially at night. Whereas Madison had been a timid kid, covering her face through horror movies and sleeping with a nightlight on. Kennedy had loved the blackness of the night. She loved darkness and barely being able to see her hand in front of her face. Now that she was surrounded by darkness all the time, she would have to grow to love it once more. Right now she sought serenity in the woods, away from people, traffic and other intrusive sounds. She wanted to reclaim some of the peaceful feeling that nature had inspired in her in the past and she wanted to share a little bit of her experiences in the country with Malik.

"And I can't believe you've never gone camping before. You haven't lived until you've slept beneath the stars and eaten food cooked over an open flame. When I was a little girl, I dreamed about marrying a lumberjack named Billy Braun, and spending the rest of my days chopping wood and fishing in a river."

"You are absolutely crazy, but you know something?" Malik asked, his arms circling her waist.

"What's that?"

"That's why I find you so damned sexy."

"Stop it." Kennedy giggled.

"Nah, girl, it's true. You are so sexy. This gorgeous body, the way you talk and laugh. Kennedy, you are incredibly hot."

"I thought you said I was crazy?" Kennedy asked, her laugh deep and throaty as she turned around to face Malik.

He pulled her shades from her face. She immediately closed her eyelids, a habit she'd developed since she'd lost her sight. He kissed her lids, one at a time, over and over until she opened them.

"Your eyes are stunning. I never know what color they're going to be when I look into them."

"I wish I could see you. Sometimes I wish I could look back into your eyes, just for a moment," Kennedy answered.

"You do see me, better than anyone I've ever known."

Malik kissed Kennedy deeply and felt his heart swell inside him. His body responded, as well, just as it always did when he touched her or even thought about touching her.

"We need to unpack and get settled," Kennedy protested, even though her hands were running up and down Malik's back and rear, pulling his body closer to hers.

"Not right now."

Standing in front of a crackling fire, the warmth caressing their bodies, there was no place that either of them would rather be. There was nothing that either of them would rather be doing than touching one another and getting lost inside their passion.

Inside the cabin, the light from the fireplace created a soft sensual glow. Malik reached behind Kennedy's head, removing the clip that held her hair in a neat ponytail. He shuddered as her thick mane fell around her shoulders, covering his hand. For a moment he buried his face in the side of her hair, the fragrant scent driving his senses to distraction. He cupped her left cheek with his free hand, pulling her face closer to his. He brushed his lips across hers, the electricity of their contact sending shivers through his body. He had never felt so alive in the arms of another woman. With Kennedy it felt as if every nerve ending was alert and attentive, waiting to be pleased by her. Malik knew that he had gone too far and fallen too deep.

On their second night at the cabin, Kennedy guided Malik step-by-step through the process of building a tent in the clearing behind the cabin. It was his first attempt and after an hour of giggling and mishaps, he erected a hexagon-shaped tent using a three-pole, pin-and-ring and shock-cord system. His work was so fine it could have won him the scout award.

"See, I told you that you could do it. You city boys really need to get out more." Kennedy laughed.

"This nature crap ain't hard. What else you got for me, huh? Want me to build a fire using two sticks? How about I catch a fish with a spear?"

Kennedy giggled, certain that if she asked, Malik would do both of those things and more. Instead, she handed him a torch lighter and he lit the pieces of wood that she'd instructed him to place within a circle in the clearing. Impressed with himself, Malik roasted a few marshmallows on sticks and fed Kennedy the sticky hot treat with his fingers.

"Tell me what the sky looks like tonight," she said.

Malik stared out into the blackened night for several minutes, silently gazing upon the heavens. He had a hard time finding the words to describe the vision.

"It looks like you," he said at last. "It's black and beautiful, bright and open. It seems like it goes on and on forever. Its beauty won't ever end."

He pulled Kennedy to her feet, picking her up off of the ground in his arms. He slowly turned around in a circle, his head titled backward and his eyes directed toward the firmament. He gently returned her to the ground, but she felt like she'd never come down again.

"This feels like forever," Kennedy said, kissing Malik's chin softly.

Malik pulled the heavy green cardigan Kennedy wore over her head, freeing her arms and body. He wanted to see her and feel her skin against his. He never tired of looking at her beautiful body, slim and toned, yet soft and supple in the places where a woman should be. He'd never had a desire for only one body type or shape of a woman, but found beauty in a wide variety of sizes and figures.

Kennedy's body, however, defied description or comparison. He realized that no matter how many other women he would come to meet for the remainder of his life, he would always draw comparisons between them and Kennedy, fair or not.

Her C-cup breasts were full and round, heavy in his hands. Her stomach held a little extra flesh, weight she admitted to having put on since the accident and vowed to shed. He hoped she didn't. He loved to squeeze the inch around her midsection and he loved the way that area felt against his body. The roundness of her hips as he glided his hands up and down them when she rode him drove him crazy, as did the feel of her thighs pressed against the side of his face when he dined on her. There was not one aspect of Kennedy's body that did not entice and excite him and each time they made love, he strove to give every inch of her equal and unparalleled attention.

"Can I make love to you right now, Kennedy?"

Malik loved to ask her that question because he

wanted to always know that she was wanting him just as much as he wanted her—all of the time.

"Yes, Malik. I want to make love with you," she responded, giving him all the permission his heart needed to move forward.

Malik unzipped the double-person sleeping bag they'd brought with them and spread it out on the grass in front of the tent. He lay down on his back, pulling her down with him across the top of his body. His mouth sought hers again and he surrendered himself to her expert kiss. He had never before found much pleasure in kissing. Perhaps it was because he had yet to kiss a woman who approached it as an art. Kennedy professed that it was Malik's mouth that propelled her to claim it with so much artistry. Whatever the reason, he reveled in the undulating pressure of her tongue as it stroked his, the way she glided it across the roof of his mouth causing sensations to erupt that he did not know were even possible.

She was wearing the white lace thong he'd bought her. It was his first trip to the lingerie section of a store. Never before had he been prompted to buy a woman underwear, perhaps because he had never before felt this close to a woman, not even the one he'd thought he was going to marry several years ago. Now, it seemed like the most natural thing in the world for him to do.

He gazed at the center of her. He was convinced that there was not one inch on Kennedy's body that was not pleasurable to look at, and that region was no exception. He bent his mouth down to kiss her opening and she gasped. Her sounds of delight drove him to linger longer than he'd intended to. He explored her with his tongue, slowly and deliberately until she begged for him to stop.

"No, go deeper," she cried.

He obliged as he always did because he'd come to think of pleasing her as his life's work and there was no greater duty he'd rather take on. He worked her into such a frenzy, kissing, sucking, licking and lapping until he was certain that her screams would wake every animal in the forest. Their lovemaking was as intense as it always was, as they gave themselves over completely to each other without reservation. Afterward, Malik stroked the side of Kennedy's face as he stared up at the bevy of stars that blanketed their love nest.

"When you were a little boy what did you want to be when you grew up?"

"A fireman. I thought I was going to spend the rest of my life running into burning buildings, chopping down flaming doors and carrying people out, five at a time, in my big strong arms. I wanted to be a hero who everyone loved and depended on."

"So what happened?"

"I don't know. I guess you grow up and you realize that there aren't any such things as heroes. All there is are people trying to live their lives the best way they can. I kind of bounced around from job to job for a while and then when I landed at Stillwater, it was like I was finally doing something to help people. It was a little bit like fulfilling my dreams. I mean, I know it's not much, what I do. It doesn't require any particular skills or intellect, but sometimes it feels like I've helped somebody. Right now, that's enough for me."

Kennedy smiled silently, her head resting against Malik's chest. She listened to the steady rhythm of his heartbeat and wished that she could have a little bit of that feeling he described. She wanted to know that in some small way she had helped or impacted someone, too. Being a financial analyst didn't quite do it for her, but it was all that she knew how to do.

"Every day I'm just thankful that I was able to find something to do with my life, something I'm good at. Otherwise, those streets could have eaten me alive," Malik mused.

"I think that the only difference between a successful person and a person who gets lost to the streets is that one of them stopped dreaming."

"Maybe you're right about that. I dreamt about you and look what happened," Malik said, covering her lips with his own.

"You've practically moved in with her. What gives?" Malcolm asked as he crunched noisily on an extra-large plastic green bowl of Corn Flakes.

"I'm not about to move in with Kennedy."

"Not that I'm knocking your hustle…I mean, she's got her own money and with her condition, well, I guess she's pretty needy right now, huh?"

Malik folded his uniform pants and placed them in a blue duffel bag. He considered his brother for a moment. Malcolm, three years his senior, had always been blunt. And he did not hesitate to share his opinions, even when they were unsolicited and unwanted.

Malcolm never lied about his emotions or his behaviors. For him, there was no point in putting in the effort it took to pretend or to cover his tracks. Perhaps that was why Malcolm's life was plagued with problems. When Malcolm decided that he no longer wanted to be with the mother of his first child, Jacob, he packed and left. He'd been brutally honest about the fact that he'd found someone new. When the mother of his second child, twelve-month-old Star, suspected he was cheating, she confronted him. Although her suspicion was based on no physical or tangible evidence, he acknowledged that she was right on target without apology.

Malcolm was not a bad man. In fact, he was giving and reliable by nature. However, with two scorned baby mothers on his back, hell-bent on making him pay for not wanting them anymore, and his only marketable skill being that of a laborer, Malcolm's honesty had left him broke and at their mercy.

Unfortunately, both of his former girlfriends had hated him. They tag-teamed him, dragging him into court for child support, denying him access to the children and otherwise making his life a living hell. Right now Malcolm was five thousand dollars behind in payments and had already served three months in jail for nonpayment of support. Things weren't looking any better these days. Malcolm was out of work once again. That was why he was staying with Malik.

"You say the dumbest stuff sometimes, man," Malik said finally.

"Just calling it like I see it," Malcolm shrugged.

"Yeah, but the problem is you don't always see with twenty-twenty vision, feel me? Kennedy is a beautiful woman, and I enjoy spending time with her. Period. I don't care about her money, her education, her blindness or anything else for that matter. She's good people and I'm going to be there for her, to help her through all this for as long as she wants me to. Simple as that. Now, instead of concentrating on what I'm doing, I'd suggest you try to get your life in order."

"Whatever, man," Malcolm grinned as he gave his brother a slap on his back.

Malik knew that his brother meant him no disrespect. Malcolm's troubles had just led him to become a cynical man who was always on the lookout for the *gotcha* in life.

Malik left the apartment, eager to get back to Kennedy. He knew that he had sugarcoated their situation to Malcolm, but he couldn't dare put into words what was happening to him. For Malik, Kennedy was a breath of fresh air. For the first time in his life, he felt like he mattered to someone. Her inability to see his face and his physical features had somehow allowed her to see into the very core of who he was. She had touched that part of him so profoundly that he finally felt alive.

Malik recognized their differences, and in his heart believed that there was probably not much of a future for them. He still couldn't make himself walk away. He meant what he said to Malcolm. He would stay put until time ran out for them. What he didn't realize was that the end of their road would come sooner than he expected.

Chapter 15

"Malik, I'm not playing with you. Tell me where we are going," Kennedy demanded.

"I'm not telling. You're going to have to beat it out of me. You're always kidnapping me and taking me to the middle of the woods and stuff. Now it's my turn."

Malik drove a rented car expertly down the busy streets of D.C. Kennedy leaned back, her head relaxed against the headrest. The radio was tuned in to an oldies but goodies station and she hummed along with tunes that she'd grown up listening to her parents sing and watching them dance to. Despite her protests, she enjoyed being whisked away by

Malik. She had the utmost faith in him. She trusted that he would not take her anywhere that she didn't want to go. He'd already taken her spiritually to places she had never imagined and physically to heights that she had never known existed. She still marveled at their lovemaking, each time discovering depths of pleasure and expression that surprised her. Warning bells were ringing in the back of her mind, as she recognized the fact that she had fallen hard and fast for him, but right now, she didn't care to listen to them. All that mattered was the present and the fact that while God had seen fit to take so much from her, He, in His infinite wisdom had also seen fit to give her so much in return. Malik was no doubt in her mind the reason why she made it through those dark days and she had every intention of holding on to the sunshine he gave her for as long as she could.

Kennedy dozed off without realizing she was even sleepy. She felt the car come to a stop and after a few seconds, began to stir.

"Malik?" she called out.

"I'm here," he said. "I was just sitting here watching you sleep. You're beautiful."

Malik leaned over and kissed Kennedy softly.

"Thank you, baby. Are we here yet?"

"Yep. Wait right there for a minute, though," he said.

The car chimed when he opened the door. He

climbed out of the driver's seat and shut the door behind him. Kennedy waited, listening for any telltale signs that would provide a clue as to where she was. In the months since the accident she had come to rely upon her other senses, especially that of sound, when it came to getting through daily tasks. Her hearing had become extremely acute and even from inside her apartment, she could tell what time of day it was by the sound of traffic and other noises coming from the outside.

Her sense of smell had also intensified as she grew dependent upon it to tell her things like what foods were being placed in front of her and who had just entered a room. The various smells of the soaps that people used, cologne that they wore and the products they applied to their hair were her guides. Unfortunately, today either her senses were extremely dull or she was in a vacuum because there were no hints. Wherever they were, it was a place where dogs weren't allowed because Malik had made her leave poor Muppet at a kennel.

The passenger side door opened and Kennedy turned toward the rush of air that greeted her.

"Come on, babe," Malik said.

He reached down and took Kennedy by the forearm. He helped her from the vehicle.

As Kennedy exited the car, her arm looped through Malik's, she inhaled sharply.

"Smells like air…all I smell is air. A lot of it. Where are we, Malik?"

"Just trust me," he said, kissing the back of her hand.

Malik led Kennedy through an empty field and into a large building that served as a hangar. Kennedy could hear voices as soon as they entered. They came to a stop before a group of people.

"Reginald, this is the little lady I was telling you about. Kennedy, meet my cousin, Reginald," Malik said.

"Hello, Kennedy, it's a pleasure to meet you."

"Likewise," Kennedy said with a smile, extending her hand.

Reginald shook her hand and held on to it.

"My cousin here forgot to mention how beautiful you are, Miss Kennedy. Guess he was scared that I'd steal you away from him."

"Well, if I don't find out what Malik is up to right about now, you just might get your chance," Kennedy joked.

"Woman, just relax and follow the man outside, would you?" Malik scolded.

They exited the building from the opposite side of where they'd entered and walked several feet across rocky terrain. They stopped in front of a small shed.

"All right, Miss Kennedy. I'm going to need you to slip into this jacket," Reginald ordered.

Kennedy followed instructions. After putting on the jacket and waiting while Malik zipped it for her, she heard the sound of metal clicking and of other fabric being zipped.

"All right, now, this might feel a little awkward your first time, but you'll get used to it," Reginald said.

"Malik," Kennedy called breathlessly.

"I'm right here."

"Are we about to do something crazy?" she asked.

There was no disguising the excitement in Kennedy's voice. Without knowing where they were or what they were about to do, she was turned on. Her willingness to step outside of the safe predictability of her life was one of the things about her that attracted Malik to her. He took her into his arms.

"We're going to strap on a pair of wings, jump off of a very big hill and glide slowly down into a valley like a beautiful swan with her friend the bald eagle by her side. Do you trust me?" he asked.

Kennedy pressed her lips to his softly.

"Yes, I do." She smiled.

"Good. I'm going to take you on the ride of your life, and I want you to trust that you'll be safe. Know that I'm going to take care of you, okay?"

With that, Malik released Kennedy and helped her get into the rest of her gear. He strapped a helmet onto her head, then secured his own.

Reginald gave them a few more instructions before giving them the okay to launch. They would be using a foot-launching technique from a hill as opposed to either tow-launching from a ground-based tow system or aero-towing from behind a powered aircraft. Malik had done all the techniques before.

Reginald assisted them strap into the hang glider. Theirs was a simple craft consisting of an aluminum-framed fabric wing. As the pilot, Malik was mounted on a harness hanging from the wing frame. He would exercise control over the craft by shifting body weight from side to side. Kennedy was secured next to him, free to just enjoy the ride.

When they fell into a quick trot along the rocky terrain, Kennedy held on to the bar in front of her tightly. Her pulse raced and she grew light-headed from anticipation. The moment that she felt the ground give way beneath her feet was the single most exhilarating of her life. The wind smacked their faces, taking her breath away. Kennedy screamed with pleasure, gripping the bar even more tightly as they sailed away into the atmosphere. Her stomach lurched and her heart threatened to beat right out of her chest, yet with Malik by her side, she truly felt like she could fly forever.

"Do you plan to have children someday, Malik?"
"Where did that come from?" Malik asked.

He looked up from Kennedy's feet, nail polish brush dipped in cherry blossom paint poised midair. It was a Sunday evening, the day after they had gone hang gliding. Twenty-four hours later, Kennedy still felt like she was flying and pressed Malik to know when they would get to do it again. He'd teased her that he hadn't done so bad for an urban city boy, as she liked to call him, before promising that he'd take her out again as soon as he could schedule time on his next day off from work.

After spending the day lying around in one another's arms, Malik had offered to give Kennedy a manicure and a pedicure. It was a skill he'd picked up from childhood when his big sister, LaToya, forced him and his brother, Malcolm, to play salon with her. Malcolm refused to touch anyone's feet so he always got to be the shampoo person, but Malik actually liked applying the polish and little designs onto LaToya's toenails.

"Just curious," Kennedy shrugged. "Answer me."

"That's a hard question. I mean, sure I'd love to have kids, start a family with a woman, but I've seen so many people jack that up. People start off deep in love and the kids come along and before you know it, the love is replaced by demands and then anger. I look at people like my brother, Malcolm, and it makes me think twice."

"Well, I think you'd be good with children," Kennedy complimented.

"Yeah, but the question is, would I be good to them? What if things don't work out with the mother, what then? I don't want to be a weekend dad. Kids deserve more than that. Growing up, my parents were one of the few couples on the block who were still together. Isn't that sad? I mean, I could count on one thing growing up, every day, and that was that my dad was coming home at nine o'clock every night with his newspaper tucked under one arm and his lunch bag under the other. That means something to me."

"I guess that's the one thing you and I have in common. I don't know what would have happened if my parents weren't together. Although I guess I never really thought about it because I didn't know any kids whose parents were divorced. I did know one girl whose mother had died, but she had her father and a nanny who was just like a mother."

"You were so sheltered," Malik said, as if he'd just suddenly realized the fact.

"You say that like it's so horrible. At least I got to just be a kid. So many children today have to act like adults before they even reach double digits. That's not right."

"No, it isn't. That's one reason why I've been thinking about doing something about it," Malik said hesitantly.

He had not shared his idea with anyone, knowing

that it was a dream that many people in his limited social circle would laugh at. Since he'd met Kennedy, he'd been thinking about it more and more and lately it didn't seem so far-fetched.

"Doing something like what?" Kennedy asked.

"I've always thought that if kids had someplace to go, to keep them occupied, they could have a better chance at escaping some of the B.S. out there on the streets."

"That's true. I mean, you hear studies and stuff all the time about that very thing. So what were you thinking of doing?"

"Well, see, that's just it. I don't think the studies really go deep enough into the problems. I mean, a lot of kids either don't have two parents, some don't even have one, or others have parents that don't really give a damn. They're too busy working or out there living their own lives to give their kids what they need. See, it's more than just about having a place to go. There are recreational centers sprinkled here and there. Kids go to those places and they shoot basketballs around, play ping-pong or what have you. Now, don't get me wrong. That's great and all, but it's not enough. There needs to be a place where kids can go to have fun and learn at the same time. A place where they can explore computers, get hands-on experience in different trades like automotive and electronics. A place where they can get tutored by professionals and learn specialized skills like culinary arts or interior decorating."

"Go on," Kennedy said.

She'd leaned forward, closer to Malik so as not to miss one single word that he was saying. He was fueled by her enthusiastic eagerness and he rushed ahead, surprising even himself at just how much thought he had given his ideas.

"What I'm proposing would almost be like a school in some respects, but it would be free. It would be situated in an area where there was a lot of public housing and poor people—the ones who need the help more than anyone else. It would be a state-of-the-art facility and it would offer a wide variety of programs. Things like mentors and cultural activities. I'd solicit professionals in various fields to donate their time on a rotating basis. Basically, all of the stuff that these so-called experts have talked about for years as the leading reason why some kids excel when others fail. For teenagers there would be a workplace readiness program to help them learn not only how to apply for jobs but also how to conduct themselves once they are on the job. There'd be a college exploration program for high school kids."

"Wow. This would be an amazing thing to see happen. It's a huge undertaking, but an amazing one at the same time. Do you have any ideas about how you could bring something like that together?"

"I don't know. I've been thinking about it for so long, but I've never actually gotten to the planning stages. I mean, I don't know the first thing about teaching or instruction."

"Who says you need to know anything about that? I think it starts with the passion and you certainly have that, along with a love for kids and a desire to help people. Everything else is just icing on the cake."

"Yeah, I'd love to be able to do something like that for the community, especially around where I grew up. I don't know, Kennedy, it's just a dream. I can't even begin to see how to make it come true."

"First things first," Kennedy said, standing up.

She moved slowly toward her spare room that served as a guest room and her home office. She counted her steps to the door and then moved inside. "Come here," she called to Malik over her shoulder.

Kennedy sat down at her desk. Malik pulled up a chair next to her in front of the computer.

"First you need to know what others have done in the field. Are there other such facilities that you could model yourself after?"

Before Malik could answer that question, Kennedy fired off three more. He had to stop himself from the compulsion to sit with an open mouth, marveling at the way her mind worked. It was a force that could rival the speed of light.

They spent the next couple of hours conducting research. She gave the directions and he followed, typing in search words on the Internet and reading the hits that popped up. She instructed him on how to tap into the national registries of not-for-profit agencies, gave him step-by-step directives on how federal funding was allocated and helped him to navigate through the jumbled language of Web sites designed for start-up businesses.

"I love that you're such a smart lady," Malik told Kennedy.

"And I love that you're a dreamer," she countered.

The fact that their attributes complemented one another's was not lost on either one of them.

Chapter 16

"Mom...what...what are you doing here?" Kennedy said as she stood in the doorway.

Muppet sat diligently at her feet, staring up at the exquisite Elmira Daniels. Kennedy tied her bathrobe at her waist securely and then nervously pushed a strand of hair that dangled on her forehead. She'd snatched open the door without asking who it was, which was a bad habit Malik had often scolded her about. She'd believed it to be the Japanese food delivery person with their order of spicy Hamachi, tuna, miso soup and rice. The second she opened the door, the scent of Elmira's signature perfume accosted her senses and she realized that it was definitely not her sushi order.

"Kennedy, where are your manners? Aren't you going to ask me in?" Elmira reproached.

"Uh, sure, Mom, come in," Kennedy said, feeling like a disobedient adolescent. "Muppet, here," she commanded as she opened the door wider and stepped back to allow room for her mother to enter.

Muppet moved to Kennedy's side, continuing to regard the visitor quizzically. He sniffed at Elmira's legs as she passed him by, but did not move from Kennedy's side. Kennedy shut the door and took a deep breath.

"I can not believe this," she muttered beneath her breath.

"Well, darling, I decided that since we can't get you to come home for a while, where you belong, I'd have to come check on you. Now, how are you f—"

Elmira stopped walking and talking at the same moment as she stared at Malik, who stood barefoot just outside of the doorway to Kennedy's bedroom. The only thing he was wearing was his jeans. His chest was bare.

"Hello, Mrs. Daniels. I'm Malik—"

Malik took a step toward Elmira, extending his hand.

"Kennedy, what is going on here?" Elmira said, turning abruptly away from Malik and facing her daughter.

"Mom, I'd like you to meet my...my friend, Malik Crawford."

"Mrs. Daniels, it's my pleasure," Malik said, offering his hand again.

Elmira considered Malik for a moment before stiffly accepting his hand and giving it a brief, perfunctory shake.

"Young man...I'm sure there's a perfectly reasonable explanation for why you're in my daughter's apartment, half-dressed at this hour in the morning and I'm equally sure that I don't want to here it. Would you mind?"

"Uh, yes, ma'am. Excuse me."

Malik glanced at Kennedy, who stood stock-still, clutching her bathrobe against her body. He wanted to cross the distance and go to her, put his arms around her and ease the tension that had her frozen like a deer in a pair of quickly approaching headlights. However, Elmira's presence was commanding and her directive was not to be ignored. He turned and stepped back into the room, giving mother and daughter a few moments to talk.

"Kennedy, who is that man?" Elmira demanded as soon as Malik had shut the door to the bedroom.

"I told you, Mom, he's a friend...a dear friend," Kennedy answered.

"Well, from the looks of things there's a whole lot more than friendship going on here. Kennedy, how could you? How could you have a man sleeping up in here with you…in your condition?"

"Condition? What condition, Mother? Oh, do you mean in my blindness? How dare I sleep with a man when I can't even see?"

Kennedy walked across the room and plopped down onto the sofa. She folded her hands across her chest like a defiant child.

"Kennedy, that's not what I meant."

"Isn't it? Look, Mother, contrary to what you might think, my vision loss is not a condition. I don't have a head cold or a toothache. I can't see, Mother, and I may very well spend the rest of my life like this. Does that mean I should stop living?"

"No, dear, that's not at all what I meant," Elmira said, crossing the room toward her daughter.

Elmira stooped over in front of her, clasping Kennedy's shoulders firmly.

"Sweetheart, you have been through a trying ordeal. These past couple of months have been life-changing, I know that. That's why it is impossible for me to believe that you are in the right state and presence of mind to be carrying on with some *man*."

"Mom, Malik isn't just some man. He has been a very good friend to me. He's the one who has helped me through this ordeal, as you put it. I don't think I could have made it without him."

Elmira sat softly on the edge of the sofa next to her daughter.

"Don't be overdramatic, Kennedy. You have a family who loves you. You are the one who told us to stay away, to give you some space. We would have been here if you'd let us. You did not need to hook up with the first opportunistic hard body that came along—"

"Mother, you will not disrespect my friend in my home. Now, if you have a problem with that, then perhaps you should just turn around and leave," Kennedy said, inching to the left, away from her mother's crudeness.

Muppet's ears perked up and he eyed Elmira with curiosity. He trotted over to where Kennedy sat on the sofa, sitting in front of her protectively. Elmira sighed, shaking her head slowly as she collected her thoughts. She chose her next words very carefully, attempting to respect her daughter's wishes.

"Kennedy, sweetie, I don't want to argue with you. I just want to make sure that you're all right. That's all I came up here for. You've got to give me a little leeway. The last thing I expected to find was…well, I'm just surprised is all."

"Mother, can we not talk about this now?" Kennedy asked. "Malik?" she called.

"Fine," Elmira muttered.

Malik opened the door and stepped into the living room. He was fully dressed and draped his jacket casually over his arm.

"Yes, Kennedy?"

"I was just thinking that it must be dinnertime by now. I'm starving. Why don't the three of us go out for dinner? We don't have to go far. How about the diner?"

Kennedy smiled, but Malik saw through the mask of her pretty smile. She was distressed and his heart lurched as he acknowledged his role in that. Malik glanced at Elmira and there was no mask designed to hide her disdain. He had had no previous interaction with Elmira Daniels yet instinctively, he knew that she was not a woman he'd ever have any warm feelings for. The last thing in the world Malik wanted to do was to break bread with Kennedy's mother. Yet, there was no mistaking the expectant look on Kennedy's face. He could not say no to her.

"Sounds good to me. Would you like me to get something out for you to wear?" he asked.

Malik's eyes remained trained on Elmira's face. He derived a malicious pleasure in watching the flash of anger that passed across her elegant face at his question. It was obvious that she resented his presence in her daughter's apartment and in her life. Without even knowing him or anything about him, she disliked him. Perhaps her reaction was the normal reaction of an overprotective parent. He was not naive enough to believe that rationale, even as his mind turned it over.

Malik excused himself again, going back into

the bedroom while Kennedy, led by Muppet, entered the bathroom. Malik retrieved a pair of jeans and sweater from her closet, undergarments from one of her dresser drawers, and took these items into the bathroom to her. He felt Elmira's eyes on him each time he walked past her and he began to sweat under their intense glare.

They left Muppet at home and Kennedy walked in between Malik and her mother, her right arm looped through his left. By the time the trio was seated at Coliseum Diner, a short walk away from Kennedy's apartment, the air between them was thick with tension. Kennedy's nervous chatter was like a dull knife that cut through ineffectively.

"Kennedy, dear, have you gotten back in touch with Mr. Schenck? Those good people at Morgan Stanley are not going to hold your position forever, you know," Elmira said after taking a sip of the effervescent mineral water she'd ordered.

"Not yet, Mom," Kennedy said, her answer short and low.

"You're going back to work?" Malik asked.

He tried to keep his gaze from drifting back to Elmira, who he was certain wore a smug expression. From the moment they'd arrived at the diner, she had been trying to engage Kennedy in topics of conversation in which he would not be able to have input. Each time she would address Kennedy about situations or people he did not know, Kennedy would find a way to turn the discussion back around to neutral ground. Now, as he studied Kennedy's face, he realized that there were things that she obviously did not wish to discuss with him, despite the fact that he'd begun to believe that they shared everything.

"No…well, I'm not sure. My father and Mr. Schenck are on the alumni board of Harvard and they were talking a couple of weeks ago. Mr. Schenck sort of insinuated that he's keeping a place for me at the company, but I don't know—"

"What's not to know, Kennedy? Just because you've temporarily lost the use of your eyes does not mean that there's anything wrong with your brain. You've earned your place at that company. Isn't that right, Malik?" Elmira asked, turning her attention to Malik for the first time that evening.

"Ma'am?" Malik asked, caught off guard by Elmira's sudden interest in his opinion.

"Don't you think Kennedy deserves her place at Morgan Stanley?"

"Of course, if that's what she wants."

"What do you mean if that's what she wants? Certainly that's what she wants. She's worked hard to get where she is. I mean, it's not easy being at the top of your class at Princeton and Georgetown universities. Hard work combined with determination is what it takes and all of her life my daughter has definitely shown that that's what she's made of."

Elmira's haughty tone could not have been more apparent if she were talking about her own accomplishments. It was obvious that she saw Kennedy's drive as a direct reflection on her and she took extreme pride in her daughter's successes.

"I won't argue that. You should have seen the way she attacked her physical therapy sessions at Stillwater."

Malik felt a twinge of guilt after his comment as he reveled in the fact that he had been the only person Kennedy could stand to be around during those weeks at Stillwater. His statement had had the desired effect, piercing through Elmira's steel frame and hitting her where she lived. She was momentarily stunned into silence. Just for a moment.

"Malik, I do need to thank you for the care and concern you've shown my daughter. We do appreciate knowing that she's had someone to rely on through these trying times."

"It was my pleasure. Like I said, she's a tough cookie. She faced those daily workouts with a smile on her face, no matter how painful they became," Malik said, his smile falling on Kennedy as he reached across the table and brushed the back of her hand lightly with two fingers.

Kennedy smiled.

"So, Malik, are you an entrepreneur or something? I mean, you must be your own boss, setting your hours if you were able to take so much time away from your job to be with Kennedy during her physical rehabilitation at Stillwater."

"No, Mrs. Daniels. I'm not my own boss…not yet, anyway. I happen to work at Stillwater."

"Oh? Well, that's interesting," Elmira said, perking up for the first time in her conversation with Malik.

The meaning behind her upbeat tone was clear to Kennedy. It was obvious to her that Malik's worth had just risen a few degrees under Elmira's mistaken assumption that he was a doctor or administrator at Stillwater. Kennedy started to interject, but the waitress appeared with their meals.

"Turkey club, on whole wheat toast?" she asked.

"That's mine. I trust there's no mayonnaise and no cheese on this," Elmira stated as she eyed the platter the waitress placed in front of her.

"Just like you ordered, with a side of carrots and celery," the young woman smiled indulgently. "And who's having the turkey burger?"

Malik raised two fingers into the air.

"Okay. And that leaves grilled chicken breast on sourdough for you."

She placed the third platter in front of Kennedy. Malik reached over and turned the platter around. He poured a dollop of ketchup on the edge of the plate above the French fries.

"Fries at twelve o'clock, salad at three," he said.

Elmira watched with raised eyebrows as he tended to her daughter.

"Thank you."

"So, Malik, you were about to tell me what it is that you do at Stillwater," Elmira said before placing a small piece of carrot between her lips.

Kennedy dipped one of her French fries into the pool of ketchup, stuck in into her mouth and bent her head further toward her plate, knowing there was no avoiding the moment that was upon them.

"I'm what you'd call a transporter. Official title is client transportation services. My job is to provide mobility to the clients, transporting them around the facility, assisting when needed in the therapy sessions and whatnot. Kennedy was one of the clients in my assigned station."

"You're an orderly?" Elmira said, her voice dripping with disbelief.

"Well, that's not a term we use at Stillwater, but I guess the functions are the same."

There were several minutes of undisturbed silence as Elmira sipped her water and digested this news. She attempted to eat another bite of her club sandwich, but remarked suddenly that she had lost her appetite. Kennedy and Malik finished their meals quickly while Elmira chewed her lip.

"Let me get this," Malik said, reaching for his wallet after the waitress had placed the bill in the center of the table.

"Nonsense, Malik. I'm sure you hadn't planned on feeding me tonight," Elmira said.

Her meaning was not lost on anyone and immediately Malik bristled at her insinuation that he could not afford to pay.

"I insist," he said shortly, snatching the check from the table.

He threw three bills onto the table, overpaying purposely, and rose.

"Let's go," he said.

He helped Kennedy from her seat and guided her out of the diner. Elmira followed, remaining a few steps behind them all the way back to the duplex. At the front door of Kennedy's apartment he leaned down and kissed her cheek.

"I'll see you tomorrow," he said.

Kennedy wanted him to stay, but she wholeheartedly understood why he wouldn't. She didn't press him.

"Mrs. Daniels, it was nice meeting you," he said.

He extended his hand toward Elmira and she took it tentatively. After a brief, limp shake, she withdrew. Malik walked away, his steps heavy with foreboding.

Chapter 17

"I don't understand why you didn't just tell me about your plans to go back to work," Malik said as he chopped tomatoes for the salad he was making.

The night before, Malik had gone back to his apartment in a sour mood. Fortunately, Malcolm was not at home and he was able to sit and brood alone. He stared at the telephone off and on all evening, hoping that Kennedy would call him, yet knowing instinctively that she had her hands full. When she did call the next day, he'd already left for work. As he rolled a client down toward the lagoon for a morning stroll, his pager went off. The relief he felt at seeing her number was disturbing and he had to force himself to wait until his lunch break to call her back. Their conversation was brief, both of them apprehensive about what the other was feeling. She informed him that her mother had gone back to North Carolina on a morning flight and asked timidly if he would be coming over that evening. He replied that he would and ended the call unceremoniously.

Elmira had drilled Kennedy for most of the night about Malik, until Kennedy finally snapped and demanded that she stay out of her affairs. She knew that she had not heard the end of it, and was certain that as soon as Elmira made it back home and rallied the troops, which meant her father, she'd swoop back in for another attack. In the meantime, Kennedy just wanted to enjoy her evenings with Malik and her nights curled up in his arms.

"Malik, it's really not that big of a deal. I'm going to be doing consulting work on a part-time basis. I'll help with the training of new analysts, do some project planning, that sort of thing. It's not like I'm able to do what I used to do before the accident."

"If it's not that big of a deal, why didn't you just tell me about it, then?"

"Would you have supported me in that decision?" Kennedy asked.

"Do you have to ask me that question?"

"No, I suppose not. I'm sorry, baby. I should

have told you about it. Forgive me?" Kennedy asked, moving closer to Malik.

Malik lowered the cucumber he'd just picked up to the counter. He leaned down, kissing Kennedy gently on her lips.

"You can make it up to me later," he said suggestively, picking up the cucumber again.

"Or…I could make it up to you right now," Kennedy said as she unzipped the sweat jacket she was wearing, revealing a skimpy black lace bra.

"Aaw, that's so cute," Kennedy exclaimed, her head thrown back in laughter.

"He was the sweetest little thing standing there with his little chunky booty, naked as the day he was born," Joyce Crawford said, her voice rising above the tingling laughter of the other three women at the table.

Kennedy was seated on the screened-in porch at Malik's great-aunt's house. It was a warm Saturday afternoon, about a week after Elmira's impromptu visit. The talk that afternoon was of day camps, little league games and family barbeques in public parks. Malik's family was warming and welcoming. Her time with them gave her an even clearer picture of Malik than she had before. They told her about what kind of boy the man had been. The nagging desire to be able to see him with her own eyes tugged at her, even as she told herself that it did not matter what he looked like. The man she had come to care for was beautiful in her eyes, in spirit and in flesh. Yet, there was still the human desire to confirm what she already knew to be true with her own eyes. She wanted her passion-filled dreams to have a face. She could not stop herself from wishing that she had met Malik before she'd lost her vision. It was a wish that she knew was as futile as it was shallow.

Kennedy knew that one of the reasons why Elmira objected to her relationship with Malik was the color of his skin. Malik had once jokingly described himself to her as tall, dark and not too bad on the eyes. While Elmira had never come out and said it, Kennedy would bet her last dollar that Malik was a shade or two too brown for her tastes. As a child, Elmira had drilled into Kennedy's head that marrying a man whose skin was too dark would be the equivalent of sending a woman's soul into eternal damnation. Elmira Ellington Daniels, with skin the color of buttermilk, had married Joseph Daniels as much for his medium-brown complexion as for his promise as a cardiac surgeon. Their union had been arranged by their parents, who were long-time country club acquaintances. Elmira believed that it was impossible for a dark-skinned black man to make it in this world and for *God's sake,* she would scold, like the time she caught eight-year-old Kennedy talking to the gardener's dark-chocolate-skinned son, *think about your children.*

As Kennedy grew older, becoming more well-read in subjects of cultural and historical development of her people, she realized that her family was guilty of perpetuating the ideology of their post-slavery ancestors who recognized that lighter skin came with some measure of acceptance from white folks. It angered her to think that no matter how many centuries elapsed, black people seemed to continue to be brainwashed into believing that somehow the degree of pigmentation in one's skin made a person more or less black, more or less beautiful and more or less threatening. These were thoughts that she tossed around in her brain, but never shared with her parents because she did not believe they could ever understand the error of their ways. Even if her father, whose light-brown complexion was close to causing him to have failed the brown paper bag test himself, felt differently, he seemed to have assimilated quite well into the black bourgeoisie. Sometimes Kennedy wondered if he did, in fact, know how close he had come to not measuring up.

Kennedy listened to the laughter and banter that came from Malik's family, the camaraderie and warmth that flowed so freely from one to another moving her. Malik's parents, Joyce and Fred Crawford, may not have had all of the material trappings and social connections that her parents had, but the one thing that they did share—the thing that glowed from them—was unpretentious and uncompromised love for one another. She had never observed the type of genuine affection between her parents that Malik's parents seemed to share. Fred and Joyce Crawford spoke to each other tenderly, even when one was just asking the other to pass the salt.

Joseph and Elmira Daniels, on the other hand, were the perfect society couple. They looked good together on paper and on one another's arms. Yet Kennedy had come to understand that theirs was a perfunctory marriage in which appearances were the only thing that mattered. Sitting in the modest backyard of Malik's family, she realized that for her parents, love had taken a backseat. It was no wonder they could not understand what she felt for Malik because they had long ago forgotten—if, in fact, they'd ever known—what it felt like to have one's soul caressed.

"So Malik tells us that before your accident you were in finance?" his aunt Janie asked, pulling Kennedy from her revelry.

"Yes, ma'am. That's right. I worked for Morgan Stanley as a financial analyst," Kennedy answered from behind a napkin she held over her mouth to block the forkful of baked beans she was chewing.

"Sounds interesting. Did you handle people's investments and whatnot?"

"Not really. I dealt more with corporations."

"Oh, okay. I ask because I've been trying to figure

out what to do with this insurance money I have left from my husband's policy. He passed a couple of months ago. He was Malik's uncle, Robert."

"Yes, Aunt Janie. I remember when Malik went to Georgia for the funeral. I'm so sorry for your loss."

"Thank you, child. Yeah, when my Bobby got sick, he said to me, he said, 'Janie, I think I'm gonna want you to take me home when the time comes.' He wanted to be buried down where his momma, daddy and two of his brothers were resting. Made me promise. So that's what I did. He was a very good provider. I mean, we weren't rich or nothin', but my Bobby made sure we did all right. Both of our kids is grown and taking care of themselves now. I even got me three grandbabies. I didn't even know that Bobby was paying on these life insurance policies for me and him, but that's the kind of man he was. Now, I've got to figure out what to do with the money. My kids say I should buy myself a big house, but I keep telling them what I want with a big ole house all to myself? This little place right here is fine with me. It's where me and Bobby spent the last fifteen years of our married life, so it's just fine with me. I think I want to save the money for my grandbabies. You know, so they can go to one of those fancy colleges and become a financial analyst or something," Aunt Janie said, patting Kennedy's hand.

"That's a good idea, Aunt Janie. College is getting

more and more expensive every minute. You could go down to your bank and talk to them about putting your money somewhere that will give it the best opportunity to grow. You don't want to just put it into a regular savings account or anything like that."

"No, don't I? Shoot, in the ole days we just stuck our money under the mattress and slept tight all night knowing it was right there." Aunt Janie laughed.

By the time the daylight faded and night fell, Kennedy felt like she was home. Now she understood where Malik got it from. Even when he was away from her side for long stretches at a time, helping out at the grill or securing Aunt Janie's air conditioner unit in the window, she was comfortable. One relative or another kept her chatting and laughing all through the day and night. All day Malik's cousin Kendall played music that kept them snapping their fingers and tapping their feet, but as the sun set, he slowed the pace and mellow tunes sung by Luther Vandross and Patti LaBelle filled the air above the tiny backyard.

"Dance with me."

Malik pulled Kennedy to her feet before she could protest. In front of his entire family, he drew her close, her body pressed against his and shared a dance that carried an unspoken solemnity.

Kennedy had adjusted to her vision loss, accepting her limitations as a small price to pay for having found a man like Malik. Yet as they danced, both of them wondered if they had gone so far out on a limb that neither of them was prepared to navigate. Once again, they fought to block out the naysayers and doubts, choosing instead to concentrate on what they had.

"I'm in love with you, Malik," Kennedy said, for the first time giving sound to the words that had been living in her heart for a long time.

"How do you know that?" Malik asked.

"I know because the hole that was in my soul before I met you is now full. I know because I want more for you than I want for myself. I just know," Kennedy said.

Malik had a million questions on his mind and in his heart, yet he voiced none of them. All he could think about was that he knew exactly how Kennedy was feeling because those were his feelings that she'd just described.

"Loving you as much as I do scares me to death. I'm scared to go where you're taking me," Malik admitted.

"I'm right there with you," Kennedy whispered, her words soft against his ear.

Later that night in bed in Kennedy's apartment, they found their way to each other through the maze of questions and qualms.

"If I put this on, then I can't see you," Malik complained halfheartedly, his senses already pulsating with excitement.

He was lying naked across Kennedy's bed and

she was sitting on top of him, her bare skin glistening from the oil that he had just rubbed over every inch of her.

"That's the point," Kennedy said.

Malik hated the prospect of not being able to view her body, deriving almost as much pleasure from simply looking at her as he did from touching her. Yet he could refuse her nothing and could not even pretend that he would not succumb to her wishes. He folded and then tied the black silk scarf around his head, pulling it securely so that his vision was completely disabled.

"Now what?" he asked.

"Now, you get a chance to feel exactly what I feel when we make love," Kennedy said.

She lowered her body so that she was lying on top of Malik's body. She began kissing his face, slow, delicate kisses that teased his senses. She moved farther down, her lips brushing against his neck, her tongue dipping into the canal of his ear. Without his vision, he could not anticipate where she would visit next, and each time she retreated and then returned with more kisses, his heart jumped a little bit. She continued her journey, visiting every inch of his torso and belly. His member stood at attention, aroused beyond recognition by what she was doing to him. He was embarrassed by the primitive moans that escaped from his lips. He wanted to call her name, beg her to stop and then not to stop, but he couldn't find the ability to articulate sensible words. When her mouth reached his throbbing manhood, he lost it. He clutched the bedsheets at his sides and bit his lips, hoping that the pain would distract him from the mind-numbing pleasure. No such luck. She worked him over like a skilled courtesan, lapping and loving him until he felt like he was having an out-of-body experience. She brought him to his first climax for the evening, his life juices spilling out all over his quivering legs. He felt as if he had died and gone to heaven.

Kennedy lay fully on top of him again, covering his shivering body with hers. It took him a little while to recover, during which she continued to kiss and lick his face and neck. Kennedy waited patiently, trusting that once Malik regained control over his senses, he would take her to heights as yet untouched. She was not wrong. They sailed the night away, allowing the connection of their souls to guide the way.

Chapter 18

Kennedy was a bundle of nerves on her first day back at Morgan Stanley. Courtney, Mr. Schenck's secretary, led her to her old office where everything had remained just as she had left it except that the active deal files had been removed. Her deals had been divided up by colleagues. She had opted to leave Muppet at home, instead using a walking cane to navigate her way from the taxi and into the building's lobby, where Courtney met her.

By the end of the first day, she was much more relaxed, relying on her knowledge of finance to carry her when nerves over her condition threatened to overwhelm her. By the end of the first week, it was almost as if she had never been away.

Just as Kennedy suspected, her mother went home and had given her father an earful. Joseph Daniels called Kennedy at the office and after a few minutes of casual conversation, he informed her that her mother was very upset about her lack of forthrightness.

"What are you talking about, Daddy?" Kennedy asked.

"Since when do you keep secrets from us?" Joseph asked.

"Daddy, I don't keep secrets from you guys. I just didn't know that I have to debrief you on every step I take in my love life," Kennedy responded.

She had been suffering from a headache all day long. She was still feeling badly at the way her mother had treated Malik and, although he was reluctant to talk about it, she knew that it bothered him, as well. Knowing that her parents did not approve of him was making it difficult for her to concentrate. She'd sat at her desk for the entire morning and had not accomplished one thing. She'd been listening to an audio of a planning meeting that had been held the week before, but she could not recall one word she'd heard. Her focus was all off.

"Now, sweetheart, you know that we respect the fact that you are a grown woman now and have your own life to lead. However, your mother tells me that the young man is practically living with you. I don't understand why you wouldn't have mentioned the fact that you are in a serious relationship with someone. Perhaps there is something about this young man that you were trying to hide from us?"

"Daddy, I wasn't trying to hide anything. Malik is an honest, decent man and he's been very good to me. He's helped me out tremendously since the accident."

"Kennedy, I'm going to be frank with you. I've done some checking into your friend and, well, there may be things that you don't know about him.

"Malik Brandon Crawford, youngest child of three. Born to parents Joyce and Fred Crawford. His mother works as the head of housekeeping at a downtown D.C. hotel. And his father is a doorman for an upscale apartment complex."

"Daddy, I know all of this. What's your point?" Kennedy asked, her headache climbing two decibels on the pain scale.

"Hold on a minute, sweetie. Did you also know that Malik served six months in a juvenile detention center when he was fifteen years old and later dropped out of high school? There is no record of him earning a GED, either. And it seems like jail is a common vacation spot for the Crawford family. His brother, Malcolm, recently served time for nonpayment of child support, and it gets better and better. When Malcolm isn't doing time, he's a con-

struction worker, or unemployed. His sister, La-
Toya, was an unwed teen mother."

"Daddy, LaToya is now a staff sergeant in the
U.S. Marines and is happily married. Her daughter is ten years old, well-adjusted and very bright.
Look, I don't even know why I'm having this conversation with you. You have a lot of nerve
delving into Malik's family history like the C.I.A.
or somebody."

"Honey, I'm just trying to protect you."

"Protect me? No, Daddy, what you and Mommy
are doing is trying to control me. I love you both and
I respect you, but I am not going to let you run my
life," Kennedy said adamantly, slamming her fist
onto the top of her desk.

"Kennedy, your mother and I just want what's
best for you and Malik Crawford is not it. You need
to stay away from him."

As reverentially as possible, Kennedy restated
her position and ended the phone call with her
father. She was in such a state emotionally and had
physically begun feeling even worse, that she
packed up and left work early. When she arrived at
home, she went directly to bed, which is where
Malik found her that evening. Other than stating
that she'd had an argument with her father, she did
not share with him any of the details of her conversation. He suspected, however, that it was much
worse than she'd let on.

* * *

"Young man, I appreciate your meeting me here today," Joseph Daniels said as Malik pulled out a chair and took a seat.

The waiter handed Malik a menu, laid an ivory linen napkin across his legs and both men waited until he'd departed before making further conversation. They were seated inside The Box, a swank Mediterranean restaurant situated on Pimmit Drive. Joseph Daniels was dressed impeccably in a charcoal-gray Hugo Boss business suit. His receding hairline, sprinkled with a miniscule amount of gray hairs, was the only telltale sign of his age. His platinum wedding band caught the light as he reached to pick up the glass of chardonnay the waiter had poured for him before leaving the bottle on the table at his request.

"Well, Mr. Daniels, you said it was urgent. What can I do for you?" Malik asked stiffly.

There had been nothing remotely friendly about Joseph Daniels's request for Malik to meet him at The Box, and the younger man did not delude himself into believing that this would be an opportunity for them to mend fences, or get on one another's good sides. The Daniels had made it quite clear how they felt about him and the only thing that kept Malik from telling them both to kiss his behind was Kennedy.

Malik knew how much her family meant to her

and how devoted she was to them. He'd been biting his tongue for so long about them that it was numb, but he cared too much to see her hurt. The past few weeks had been emotionally draining for Kennedy and he'd been trying his best not to make her feel like she was in a tug of war between him and her parents. They were doing a good enough job of that without his assistance.

"Have some wine. It's a very good year," Joseph said.

Malik said nothing, watching as the elder man filled his glass. The muscle in Malik's temple was already throbbing with tension, but he vowed to remain calm and to listen to what the man had to say. He owed Kennedy that much.

"So, er, did you happen to mention to my daughter that you were meeting me this evening?" Joseph asked.

"No, I didn't. Should I have?" Malik asked.

"No, well, uh…I guess that's entirely up to you. I just felt that it was time that you and I talked…you know, man to man. Is that all right?"

"Sure. I don't have a problem with that. Mr. Daniels, I know we didn't get off to a very good start. I really wish that I had had an opportunity to meet your wife under different circumstances, but it didn't happen that way. I know how concerned you both are about your daughter's welfare, and I just want you to know that I would never do anything to hurt Kennedy."

Malik spoke from the heart, looking Kennedy's father squarely in the eye so that there would be no ambiguity or mixed meaning. Joseph regarded Malik for a moment, the sincerity in the young man's words apparent to him.

"I appreciate that, Malik. You seem like a decent young man, and I know that you care about my daughter. I hope you can understand how difficult it is for a father to accept the young men who come into his baby girl's life. One day, God willing, you'll have a daughter and you'll be sitting on the other side of this table, in my seat."

"I understand, sir."

"Yes, well, in the meantime, it's very important to me that you understand that I hold no personal ill will against you. From what Kennedy has told us, her mother and I, you've been nothing but honorable and respectful. We sincerely appreciate the assistance you've given our daughter during this trying time."

"I know I don't have to tell you this, but Kennedy is a strong, tough woman. She would have landed on her feet without me," Malik said.

"Yes, well, be that as it may, you were there for her and we appreciate it. Kennedy is thriving. She's working back at Morgan Stanley, limited duties on a part-time basis, true, but we believe it's just a matter of time before she's back to her old self. Did she tell you that the specialist she saw when she was at home with us gave her some very encouraging news?"

"Yes, she mentioned it," Malik said.

He kept to himself the fact that Kennedy had told him that her parents were hell-bent on ensuring that she regained her eyesight. It was to the point that they heard only what they wanted to hear from the doctors and even from her. It was obvious to Malik that imperfection had no place in the Daniels family tree.

"So, you see, it's just a matter of time before Kennedy is one hundred percent again. She'll be back to working full-time and will pick up her life right where she left off."

Joseph took a long sip from his glass, eyeing Malik over the rim as he did so. Malik remained silent, waiting for the man to get to his point, which he was certain was not going to be as pleasant as the phony smile that had been plastered on his face since Malik sat down.

"I'll get to the point. I think that it's time that you start to take a good look at the situation, as it truly is. Now, I know that you and Kennedy have been spending quite a bit of time together. With her unable to do the things she used to do, she's been...uh, well, she's been accessible to you. However, that won't be the case much longer and perhaps now is a good time for you to acknowledge the situation."

"Sir, I'm not quite sure what you're getting at, and I would really appreciate if you would just spell it out for me," Malik said tensely.

"All right, son, let's put the cards on the table. The Kennedy you've been spending time with is not the real Kennedy. My daughter has a challenging career, which is both time consuming and growing. She is headed places and with focus and dedication, she will be a very successful woman. She has social obligations and responsibilities that also take up a great deal of her time. Now, you probably can't relate to what I'm saying, but Kennedy is not the kind of woman who has time for card games and backyard barbecues."

Malik bristled at his statement, his lower jaw pulsing as he ground his molars together.

"Sir, I know that Kennedy is a motivated, ambitious woman. That's one of the things that I like about her, her drive."

"Right. You say that now, Malik, but I doubt seriously that you understand all of the implications that go along with that. You work as an orderly, isn't that right? You work a set shift, what, thirty-five hours a week? You get two weeks vacation a year and a few sick or personal days. What you make in salary in a month Kennedy brings home in a week."

"So this is about money?" Malik said, understanding spreading slowly across his tense face.

"No, it's not just about money. When you vacation, where do you go? Do you vacation in the Pocono Mountains in Pennsylvania? Perhaps to Florida for a week or someplace like that. Kennedy has vacationed all over the globe. She cut teeth in the Turkish Islands and we have a villa in the South of France. Face it, son, you and Kennedy are worlds apart and no matter how devoted you are to her, you will never have anything real in common."

There it was. Loud and in Technicolor. On the way to this meeting Malik had nearly driven himself crazy trying to figure out what Joseph Daniels could possibly have to say to him, and what's more, how he would say it, but here it was. Now that it was out there, Malik didn't know how to respond. Part of him felt relieved as all pretenses were finally shattered. The Daniels did not now, nor would they ever, accept him as a part of their daughter's life. He knew that he should feel angry, but somehow that wasn't the first emotion that came to him. The overwhelming feeling he felt was sadness. For Kennedy, because she was a beautiful person despite having come from such ugliness and for Joseph and Elmira Daniels because they didn't even know how ugly they really were beneath the Cartier and Dolce & Gabbana masks they wore.

"Mr. Daniels, with all due respect, Kennedy is a grown woman, last time I checked. If she chooses to be with someone like me, then I think that what you feel really doesn't matter."

Malik snatched the napkin from his lap and tossed it onto his still-empty plate as he pushed his chair back from the table.

"I beg your pardon, young man, but Kennedy is my daughter, and it damned well does matter what I feel," Joseph said, banging his hand against the table.

His action drew a couple of looks from patrons seated at nearby tables. He glanced at them and returned his gaze to Malik, trying to collect his composure.

"Mr. Daniels, I think this conversation should end here, before one of us says something he'll regret," Malik said.

"How much?"

"Excuse me?"

"How much will it take to get you out of my daughter's life? Whatever it is you're after, Mr. Crawford, Mrs. Daniels and I will see that you get it."

"After? What, so now you think I'm after Kennedy's money? Are you crazy, man?" Malik stared incredulously at Joseph, his anger now replaced by absolute disbelief.

"Kennedy comes from a wealthy family and she also has a very successful future ahead of her. Don't tell me that you have any prospects of ever living the kind of lifestyle that Kennedy lives," Kennedy's father said with a sneer.

"My prospects are none of your goddamned business, Mr. Daniels. But, you can rest assured that I don't want any of Kennedy's money, and I damned sure don't want any of yours."

Malik stood up abruptly, shaking the table as he

did and causing his untouched glass of wine to tip over. The liquid spread across the table in the direction of Mr. Daniels, dripping off into his lap before he could move. Malik stormed away as the waiter rushed over to Mr. Daniels's aid.

"Malik," Joseph called after him.

His call fell on deaf ears.

Malik walked the streets for hours, his anger fueling his feet, pushing him down block after block. He did not want to go home to an empty apartment or, worse, to Malcolm's pessimism. For the first time since he'd met her, he also did not want to go to Kennedy. He could not see her right now and manage to stop the fury he felt toward her parents from spilling out in front of her. He felt dirty and demeaned and he feared how those feelings might make him act toward her. He had no idea what he would say and do when he next saw her. He needed some time on his own to sort things out.

Malik finally came to rest on a bar stool at Murphy's. He realized that he'd made a huge mistake as soon as he walked through the door and bumped into Nona Torres, who was on her way out of the establishment with two women he didn't know.

"Malik, fancy seeing you here," she chirped.

As usual, Nona looked like a million bucks. She wore all black tonight, a short tight skirt that showed off her toned, shapely legs, and a fitted V-neck sweater to which most brothers who spotted her would have shouted *have mercy* and grinned foolishly as she passed them by.

"Nona, how're doing?" Malik asked.

"Fine, now that I'm seeing your handsome face," she flirted.

Malik wanted to be annoyed, and perhaps had he not been in such a foul mood and in desperate need of a distraction, he might not have been affected by her pretty face and sweet smile.

"Same old Nona, huh? Are you always *on?*" Malik laughed.

Nona's coy smile was little-girl infectious, but Malik knew that she was in no way innocent. She was a predator in every sense of the word and as usual, she made him feel like a baby lamb being led to slaughter.

"What can I say, baby?"

The twinkle in her eye was not lost on him. She reached out and touched his arm.

"You look like you could use a drink," she replied.

"I thought you were headed out with your friends," Malik nodded in the direction of the two scantily clad women standing near the doorway.

"I've always got time for you," Nona purred.

She stepped away from Malik and spoke briefly to her girlfriends, who gave Malik the once over before sending Nona knowing glances. He resisted the urge to *baaa*.

One drink turned into two, which multiplied into

four. The music was good and the company was scintillating. Malik was feeling no pain by the time Nona suggested they go back to her place for a nightcap. She had succeeded in pushing thoughts of Joseph Daniels from his mind, which was what he wanted. What he really wanted, however, was to forget about Kennedy, as well. He wanted to forget that he'd met her, forget how she'd stirred his soul and made him want things that he could never have. He knew that Nona was not even close to being what he wanted, but she was there and there was no one telling him that he wasn't good enough to have her.

Nona shifted her car's gears to park after pulling into a space outside the townhouse she shared with a girlfriend. She leaned over to Malik, whose head was resting against the passenger-side window with his eyes closed. She laid a hand on his upper thigh and squeezed firmly, her breath causing his ear to tingle.

"I'll make you forget about whatever is troubling you, Malik," she said.

Her tongue slithered into his ear, teasing him with promises of what was to come. He tried to lose himself in the moment and to allow Nona to work her feminine wiles on him. He shut his eyes tightly, but all he could see was Kennedy. He tried to inhale Nona's scent, he moved his hands through her hair, but it was Kennedy's sweet smell that stimulated him. It was Kennedy's firm thighs he envisioned wrapped around his and her hair in which he wanted to bury his face. After several minutes of heavy petting with Nona, Malik abruptly pushed her away from him.

"Stop it, Nona," he said when she reached for him again.

"What's wrong with you?" she demanded, her desire evident in the throaty tone of voice she used.

"Look, I'm…I'm sorry. I shouldn't be here with you, like this. It's not right," Malik struggled to explain without sounding like an idiot as he adjusted his clothing.

"Damn it, Malik, I'm not proposing marriage to you. I want you. I've made that pretty clear since the day I met you and I know that you want me, or else you wouldn't be here. What is the problem? Why can't we just both get what we want and then see what happens?"

"Nona, I don't roll like that. I'm sorry that I led you on. You're a beautiful woman and a man would have to be out of his mind not to see that. But, Nona, this…this, us—I just can't do it. All it would be is sex, Nona, and I don't want to use you like that."

"Use me? What makes you think it wouldn't be me who was doing the using?" she countered.

Malik laughed and even Nona cracked a smile.

"My bad. Well, in that case, I don't want to be used by you," he said.

Malik opened the passenger door and climbed out of the car. He walked around to the driver's side and helped Nona out. He laced his arm in hers and escorted her to the front door of her apartment.

"Do you want me to call you a cab?" she asked.

"Nah, I'm going to walk a little bit…try to clear my head. Thanks, Nona."

"Don't mention it," she said, touching the side of his face lightly with the back of her silky hand.

Malik turned to walk away before his resolve crumbled beneath her fiery touch.

"Malik," Nona called after he had taken a few steps.

"Yeah?"

"I hope things work out with her," she said.

Malik considered her intuitive words and smiled slightly.

"Me, too."

Chapter 19

Kennedy had come home for the Twentieth Annual American Physicians' Dinner honoring her father for his years of excellence as a cosmetic surgeon. It was quite an achievement and although Kennedy was not in the mood to visit with her parents, still bitter over their treatment of Malik and the constant pressure they were placing on her, she knew that it was important for her father to have both of his daughters and his wife at his side.

Publicly, the Daniels were still a tight-knit unit and no matter what was going on behind the scenes, her parents strained to uphold that image. During the entire evening, Madison kept to herself, sitting in a corner and silently nursing glass after glass of white wine, the strongest thing her parents would let her have to drink. Whenever Elmira would bring someone over to introduce her to, Madison would offer a polite smile, saying little, and would roll her eyes behind her mother's back as they departed.

Kennedy had wanted Malik to accompany her to the dinner, but under the circumstances, decided against it. She still clung firmly to the hope that in time, her parents would come around and grow to at least like Malik. Something had to give because she did not know how much more she could take.

Elmira had seen fit to invite Bret Fields to the function to be Kennedy's date. Bret was the *chosen* one as far as Elmira was concerned. He remained by Kennedy's side all night, waiting on her hand and foot. While his gestures were designed out of a simple desire to be of assistance to her, she felt smothered. In fact, the three hours she spent that evening with Bret reminded her in no uncertain terms that she was handicapped and that she would never be fully independent again. Somehow, when Malik helped her, she was never left feeling that way.

Kennedy and Bret first met three years ago at a Republican Party Meeting of Friends fund-raiser that her parents had dragged her to. Their parents were both members of the club and their fathers had become golf buddies in recent years. While their courtship had not been arranged by their parents, it had certainly been coaxed along by them. Bret was a Morehouse man, a Kappa and a rising star attorney. He was also very easy on the eyes. At six feet five inches, athletic build, he was often mistaken for a male model. After graduating from Harvard School of Law, he landed an associate position at one of the most prominent law firms in North Carolina and was headed to the top with a bullet. Bret had his sights set on becoming one of the youngest Supreme Court Justices in history.

Their attraction to one another was not earth-shattering or explosive. Kennedy did not feel butterflies in her stomach when she looked at him or even when he called her the first time. Yet, there was a mutual interest that grew over time. Their backgrounds were similar and their families couldn't be happier when they became a couple. Looking back on it, Kennedy realized that their breakup was as uneventful as their relationship had been. They had been dating one another exclusively for a little over a year and, although there had been no official proposal, it was assumed that they would one day get married. However, it had also become obvious to Kennedy that Bret was not the type of man who could handle not being the only star in the show. As Kennedy's career also began to flourish, Bret became more insistent that she slow down. He didn't see the need for her to work so hard, even though he did. Kennedy soon realized that Bret wanted a woman who would be the background. When she accepted the position at Morgan Stanley in D.C., she knew that it would mean the end to their relationship. She did not hesitate for one second. It wasn't until she met Malik that she really felt valued for the whole person that she was and not what was expected for her to be.

Malik. There he was again. Always present in her thoughts, always the prevailing thought in her mind. She had never before been this consumed over a man and it scared her. She had not truly realized how important he had become in her life and now that that relationship was being threatened, she felt a sense of panic. To a large degree, that is what kept her at odds with her parents because she had grown so tired of their constant interference in her life, be it outright demands or thinly veiled threats. Yet there remained the nagging notion that they may be right. Perhaps it was too much to expect that she and Malik could build a life together. Maybe their differences were, indeed, too great. Kennedy, fiercely determined to believe in the possibilities of love, would never utter those words aloud. However, that did not stop them from creeping into her thoughts every now and then.

"So, Kennedy, your mother tells me that you're planning to start your own foundation for the visually impaired. I think that's great," Bret said.

Kennedy's attention was pulled away from the

couple seated behind their table. While she could not see their faces, she had been eavesdropping on their conversation. The man had just proposed and through tears, the woman accepted. The love they felt for one another was undeniable as they discussed plans for their future. Kennedy could not help but feel a boulder-sized and bitter-tasting lump of jealousy settle within her chest.

"My mother talks too much," she said without humor.

Bret laughed.

"She reminds me of my grandmother. She's my biggest cheerleader."

"Now that's a funny thought, Elmira as a cheerleader." Kennedy laughed sardonically. "Seriously, though, the foundation is my mother's idea. I told her that it's a great idea and that I'd be happy to help out in any way I can. Somehow her feverish little brain translated that into something else."

"You know how our mothers are. They think we can do anything, rule the world, even. Sometimes they want so much," Bret said wistfully.

He stared into his glass without speaking for a moment. Kennedy picked up on the slightly melancholy tone in his voice, something that was very unusual for the Bret she had known.

"Don't tell me *Wonderboy* is feeling overwhelmed in his quest to take over the galaxy?" she joked.

"Never that," Bret laughed. "Let me get that for

you," he said, as Kennedy reached for a piece of sourdough bread from the basket in the center of their table.

"Bret, you've got to stop," Kennedy said at last.

"Stop what?"

"Stop treating me like a crippled old woman. I can't take it."

"I'm sorry, Kennedy…I just, I think it's amazing how you're dealing with this."

"It's not like I have a choice, now, is it? Look, Bret, I know my mother has told you everything about my condition, because like I said earlier, she talks too much. But despite what she and my father think, I have no idea whether I will regain my vision or not. Consequently, I have to take care of myself. I have my whole life ahead of me, and I can't sit around waiting for other folks to do it for me. So trust me when I say that I'm capable of buttering my bread and many other neat little tricks. Now, if you can back off just a little bit, we can enjoy the rest of our dinner together. What do you say?"

Bret contemplated her for a moment, a smile playing at his lips.

"Did I tell you how beautiful you look today?" Bret asked suddenly, changing the subject.

Kennedy smiled. Bret had always been complimentary of her looks. She would not call him superficial exactly. It was just that he was the kind of person who placed a great deal of significance on appearance. He dressed impeccably at all times, even when he was just going to the gym or the club to play racquetball. Every one of his friends were handsome, well-dressed men and their girlfriends were all knockouts, whether by nature or by design. Sometimes, when in the presence of so much concentrated physical beauty, Kennedy felt like she was a raggedy little orphan who had been dropped off in a land of make-believe princes and princesses.

She ignored his compliment. They chatted for much of the evening and slowly Kennedy felt the pressure from the past few weeks being pushed into the far corner of a closet at the back of her consciousness. She began to relax and actually had a good time talking with Bret. They danced a few times to the music played by the mini orchestra, and she settled into his arms. She got a warm, familiar feeling from being close to Bret and she remembered how simple and comfortable their life together had been. Being with someone who society expected you to be with was so much easier. That was a fact that Kennedy could not deny. However, the problem was how to get your heart to reconcile with that.

At Bret's insistence, he drove her back to her parents' house that evening. During the ride they laughed and joked about old times.

"How long are you going to be in town?" he wanted to know.

"I'm leaving tomorrow," Kennedy informed him. "Why?"

"I'd like to see you again. Any chance you can stick around a little bit longer?" he asked.

Kennedy considered it for a moment, but that moment was fleeting. Thoughts of Malik came crashing back into her mind.

"No, I need to get home," she said without offering further explanation.

"I understand. You know, I'm going to be spending some time in D.C. in a couple of weeks. I've got an arbitration coming up. Maybe I'll give you a call when I get up there."

"That'd be nice, Bret," Kennedy responded.

Bret's kiss was not unexpected, nor was it unwelcomed. His lips felt strangely comfortable against hers. She remembered their lovemaking with fondness, but also knew that it lacked the untamed passion she shared with Malik. Malik had ruined her for other men. The mere touch of his hand caused her skin to erupt and there was no comparison to that feeling.

A few days later, thoughts of Bret still lingered on Kennedy's mind. There was something so attractive about the lack of conflict that could be found with a man like Bret. As the days passed, she felt Malik moving further away from her like an inevitable and natural progression. The words they shared were short and usually marked by tension.

Early one morning, as Kennedy showered, the ringing telephone sparked yet another argument.

"Malik, would you get that, please," Kennedy called from the shower.

The door to the bathroom was slightly ajar. Malik, who was seated on the sofa reading the instructions for the computer screen reader Kennedy had just purchased, glanced at the caller identification device, which provided no information as to who was calling.

"It's a blocked number," he called.

"Pick it up, please. It's probably Skyy calling from Italy. I'll be right out," Kennedy responded, turning the shower controller to the off position.

As she stepped out of the shower, wrapping a thick, fuzzy towel around her body, she heard Malik slam the phone receiver down onto its cradle. She came out of the bathroom.

"Who was it?" she asked.

Malik did not respond immediately.

"Malik?" she called as she moved toward the living room.

"It was your mother," he said.

There was no mistaking the hostility in his voice.

"What'd she say to you?"

"Do you mean after she asked who this was answering her daughter's phone? Oh, then she said she'd call back when and if I was out earning my own money, if that day ever came."

Kennedy's shoulders drooped and her head sagged as she realized that her hopes for a pleasant day with Malik, devoid of the tension and discord, had just been blown into a million pieces.

"I'm sorry, Malik," she said.

"Sorry for what? You didn't say it," he said tightly.

"I'm going to call her back," Kennedy said.

"For what? It's not going to change anything, Kennedy. Not one bit," Malik said.

He tossed the instruction manual he'd been reading down onto the sofa. He ran his hand through his hair, his frustration clear in his every movement.

"Kennedy, I don't want to do this. Not today. I don't want to go through all of this again. I'm tired of it, Kennedy."

"Are you tired of me?" she asked.

Malik did not respond. He couldn't find the words to tell her how torn apart he was inside. He loved her yet the past few weeks had eaten at his heart and soul. He didn't know how much more he could take. The room became confining, as if suddenly transformed into a prison from which there was no pardon and no possibility of escape. He was in a cell in which it did not matter whether he was guilty or innocent, good or evil, honorable or immoral. He had been tried and convicted on the basis of social class.

Malik trained his eyes on Kennedy, the face and body of a woman who had stolen his heart without even trying. She was in so much pain and turmoil, and he could not shake the guilt he felt over that. She had been trying so hard to do what everyone wanted her to do. She was caught in the middle of a war not of her making, and she was the main casualty.

Malik's next words were out of his mouth before his brain had calculated the implications of them, but once they were said, there was no turning back.

"We need to take a break for a while, Kennedy…some time apart, just to sort some things out for ourselves," Malik said.

Kennedy's face changed, growing darker and more strained.

"What are you saying, Malik?" she asked.

"I'm going to go back to my place for a few days."

The air was charged with tension and Kennedy warred with her thoughts and emotions. Part of her wanted to beg him to stay, but there was another part of her that was tired. It was that part that won out.

"Fine, Malik," Kennedy said after a quiet moment.

She walked away from Malik, counting her steps to her bedroom. She closed the door behind her and leaned against it. Kennedy willed herself not to cry. She had shed enough tears over the past few months, and she was determined not to let another fall from her eyes. However, after several long minutes had passed, and she heard the front door shut and lock, the tears began to fall and she could no longer hold her emotions in check.

* * *

It was almost three o'clock in the morning when Kennedy turned the key in the lock of her apartment door. She stepped inside and stood in the entryway for a moment. Muppet remained by her side, waiting anxiously for some command from her.

"Malik," she said softly, not asking but simply acknowledging that he was there.

He wouldn't allow himself to be amazed that she had sensed his presence. He didn't feel the need to respond, either. Kennedy moved farther in the apartment, shutting the door behind her. She made her way into the living room, feeling a profound sense of darkness around her. It was a strange sensation since she had been unable to see virtually anything for months, yet tonight seemed unusually dark to her.

"Are you sitting in the dark?" she asked.

"Yes," Malik answered.

It was the first sign of life he'd offered.

"Why?"

Malik turned on the lamp next to the sofa.

"Is that better?"

Kennedy moved to the sofa and sat down beside him. It had been almost four days since they'd had their last argument, when Malik had announced that he was going back to his apartment for a while. They had not spoken, yet both of them had thought of nothing else. Kennedy knew that the moment would come when they'd have to get things out into the open and discuss what was happening between them. She just didn't know that that moment would happen in the middle of the night.

"How long have you been sitting here in the dark?" she asked.

Malik ignored her question. He couldn't bring himself to face her.

"Who is he?" he asked simply.

"Malik—" Kennedy began.

"No, just answer me," he snapped.

"He's nobody."

"Nobody, huh? Ha." He laughed. "That's pretty funny to me. How is it that you'd hang out until three o'clock in the morning with nobody. He sure didn't look like nobody."

"What are you talking about, Malik?"

"I saw you, Kennedy. I saw you leave with him…hours ago. I saw the way you let him wrap his arm around your waist. I saw you get into his car. I *saw* you."

Kennedy replayed the moments when she met Bret downstairs that evening. He'd been standing beside the door when she and Muppet came out. He had put his arm around her waist and walked her to his car. He'd also leaned down and kissed her lips. It was a short kiss, but she had not objected to it. She'd kissed him back. The meaning in Malik's pained tone was clear to her.

"Malik, let me explain."

"What's there to explain, Kennedy?"

"It's really not what you think. Bret and I used to be together before you and I ever met. He's in town on business and he just stopped in to check up on me. We're friends, Malik."

"Yep, that's exactly what it looked like to me," he said sarcastically.

Kennedy reached out, aiming for where she thought Malik's face was. She wanted to touch him as she had been longing to do for the past four days. However, he intercepted her hand, pushing it away harshly.

"Bret is an old friend, but that was a long time ago. There is nothing between us anymore," Kennedy explained.

She was telling the truth. Over dinner back at Bret's hotel, she had made that much clear to him.

Bret had accepted her rejection graciously and they'd even sat around for a long time continuing to talk about the past, and their respective futures. When he brought her home, they parted as friends. She was confident in her decision that she did not desire to resume a relationship with Bret, despite the fact that Elmira was pushing for it. Her heart belonged to Malik and even if things did not work out between them as she hoped, she knew that Bret was not the man of her dreams.

"Malik, don't act like this," Kennedy chided when Malik scoffed at her statement.

"Like what, Kennedy? Oh, I get it. I shouldn't act like the jealous boyfriend because I'm not your boyfriend, right? What am I, then, Kennedy? Why don't you tell me what I am to you? And while you're at it, why don't you tell me how I should act? You seem to know everything about how I feel so tell me what you want me to do."

"Damn it, Malik, I don't know anything anymore. Everything is so messed up right now with you, with my parents. I don't know anything," Kennedy said, unable to stop the waterworks from forming again.

"You used to know me and you used to know that you loved me. What happened to that, Kennedy?" Malik said.

His voice, too, was choked with emotion. She reached out and found his face.

"I do love you, Malik. That is the one thing that I do know."

"But it's not enough, is it, Kennedy? It will never be enough. I will never be enough for you. I don't have a shiny new Porsche like old boy or a membership to anyone's country club," Malik said, pulling Kennedy's hands roughly away from his face.

"I don't care about those things, Malik, and you know that."

"Do I? Just like you, I don't know anything anymore, either. No, let me correct that. I knew from the beginning that we were wrong for each other, but I tricked myself into believing that none of that mattered."

"Malik, don't say that."

"It's true, Kennedy, and you know it. You know that no matter what, your family will never accept me. To them I will never be good enough. I was good enough to read to you, to help you bathe, to serve you but that's all I'll ever be good enough for and deep down inside, Kennedy, you are just like them, aren't you?"

"How dare you say that to me, Malik? How dare you talk to me this way?" Kennedy shouted.

"Oh, I'm sorry, Miss Daniels. I must have forgotten my place for a moment. It won't happen again," Malik shouted back, his voice dripping with sarcasm.

"So is this what it is now, Malik. Are you mocking me? Are you throwing where I come from into my face now? Okay, fine. If this is really what you think of me, I guess I should just pay you now for all of your time and service. Is that what you want?"

Malik began to laugh, a harsh sound escaping his throat.

"See what I mean? You people think that because you have money, you're all that."

"*You people?* Exactly who in the hell is *you people,* Malik?"

"You, your father, your mother; all of you educated, social-climbing black folks who think your pedigree and your old money makes you less black than the rest of us," Malik spewed, his anger causing his blood to boil and his head to spin.

"You know what, Malik? You can just get out. I don't need you, Malik. Do you hear me? I don't need you. Get out!"

Kennedy jumped to her feet, her body shaking with anger.

"Is that what you want, Kennedy?"

Malik sprung to his feet, as well, grabbing Kennedy's shoulders and drawing her closer to him.

"Is that really what you want?" he whispered.

Kennedy was crying now, her tear-soaked face distorted with anger and pain. She took a step back, slapping the palms of her hands against Malik's chest. She wobbled, nearly losing her balance, but regained control.

"Get out," she screamed again.

"I'm gone," Malik said.

He made his way to the door, without looking back. He knew that if he turned around, he would not be able to walk away from her. With each step, his heart seemed to be tearing into two. He didn't stop moving. It was time. Part of him had always known that this moment would come, despite how he'd tried to convince himself otherwise. Malik tossed the keys to Kennedy's home on the small table situated just inside the entryway. This time, when he closed the apartment door behind him, he had no intentions of coming back.

Chapter 20

Malik scratched his unshaven face, stumbling to the door of his apartment as quickly as he could make it in order to stop whoever it was from beating the door down. He'd been drinking much of the day, after having called in sick to work, and had polished off a pint of Hennessey by himself. He knew that drinking himself into oblivion was not going to make him feel any better, but for once, he just didn't want to have to think. He'd fallen asleep fully clothed across his bed a few hours ago and the sound at the apartment door had dragged him reluctantly from his slumber. He snatched it open roughly.

"What do you want?" he snapped.

"Mr. Crawford, I think you know what I want. May I come in?"

Malik's jaw muscles clenched and unclenched tightly as he weighed his options. He did not feel like dealing with Kennedy's father. It was obvious that she had gone running to Daddy to tell how the big, bad hospital worker had broken her heart. Part of him wanted to just spit in this man's face and be done with the whole thing. Yet another part of him could not be disrespectful to Kennedy's father no matter how much he despised the man and all that he stood for. That was the part of him that would be in love with Kennedy for the rest of his life.

He stepped aside and allowed Joseph Daniels to enter his apartment.

"Mr. Crawford, I think that you and I got off on the wrong foot and I'm here to correct that."

Malik just stared at him without responding, eager for him to get to his point and then leave.

"I do not hold any ill will toward you personally, young man, and I want to make that clear from the start. I don't blame you one bit for the attraction you have toward my daughter. She is a magnificent young woman, and any healthy young man would be captivated by her. What you don't understand is that as a father, it is my duty to protect and nurture her. I and I only bear the responsibility of making sure that my daughters' lives are steered in the proper direction."

"With all due respect, sir, would you please get to the point."

"Yes, well, the point is that while you may think that you have my daughter's best interests at heart, there is no way on earth that you and she could work. It is criminal for you to continue with this farce of a relationship one minute longer and I am here to demand that it stops, right here and right now."

It was at that moment that Malik realized that Joseph Daniels had no idea that he and Kennedy had parted ways. Malik almost laughed out loud at the ridiculousness of this man and he would have if the entire situation wasn't so sad. He wavered between telling the man that he no longer had anything to worry about and letting him continue to talk, opening his mouth wider and wider to make room for the foot he'd later have to insert. Before Malik could reach a decision either way, the door to the spare bedroom opened and out stepped Malcolm, who appeared to have gotten an earful.

"Malik, what's going on here?" he asked with the authority of an older brother.

"Nothing, man. This is Mr. Daniels, and he just stopped by to talk about his daughter, Kennedy."

"Sounds like he's here doing more threatening than he is talking," Malcolm surmised.

He raked his eyes coldly over Joseph, from head to toe, forming an opinion in one instant.

"Look, gentlemen, I didn't come here to make

trouble. However, I have to stand by my principles. My daughter is off-limits to you, Malik. Period."

Malcolm laughed out loud.

"Check this dude out. You've got some big balls, I'll tell you that much, man. You walk into a grown man's home and proceed to tell him what he's not going to do? Boy, I'd like to be you when I grow up…ain't that right, Malik?"

"Mr. Daniels, it's time for you to leave," Malik said.

He sensed that with Malcolm's presence, this situation was going to go from bad to worse. Malcolm was hotheaded and he would not stand for someone attacking his manhood. A result of being raked over the coals by his babies' mommas and being reamed by the court system, he was a man who had reached his limits. On top of that, Malcolm had always been fiercely protective of his siblings.

"I'm not leaving until this matter is settled, for once and for all," Joseph said.

Malcolm stepped farther into the room, his face a mask of irritation and impatience. Malik moved quickly until he was standing in front of his brother, blocking his advance. He kept his back to Joseph Daniels while he locked eyes with his brother.

"I've got this," Malik said, his voice thick with meaning.

Malcolm studied his brother's calm face for a moment, the seriousness of his intentions evident.

From the moment his little brother was born, Malcolm had felt responsible for him. Malcolm knew that as a role model, he had not done a very good job of teaching Malik right from wrong. He had made his share of mistakes and was certain that he would make a few more before all was said and done. What he couldn't give his brother by way of example, he gave in support. He didn't care what Malik needed; if he had it to give, he gave it. It didn't matter what conflict or problem Malik faced. Malcolm would be at his side at a moment's notice to face it with him. During these recent months when he had been so down on his luck, in need of a place to stay and, at times, in need of financial help, Malik had been there for him. That was the type of relationship they shared.

Right now, it appeared that it was his turn to have his brother's back. Standing up to an uppity, pompous jerk was chump change in comparison to the debt he owed. However, he had to respect the fact that his brother was no longer a little boy caught in a street fight who needed protecting. His brother was a man who needed to deal with his problem. He nodded slowly, folded his arms and leaned back.

"Mr. Daniels, I'm going to walk you down to your car," Malik said.

He slipped his feet into the flip-flops that he'd left in the corner of the living room and moved, shirtless, toward the door. Joseph followed him out of the apartment and down the four short flights of stairs. They exited the building from a side door that lead directly into the parking lot. Malik spotted Joseph Daniels's sedan parked illegally in a handicapped spot. He stopped walking right beside it.

"Look, Malik. I know you're a hardworking man who could use a break. I'm going to give it to you," Joseph said.

He reached into the inside breast pocket of his suit jacket and pulled out an envelope. He extended in front of him toward Malik. Malik looked from his self-assured, smug face down to his hand several times. The rage that had been swimming within him for the past five days intensified, boiling beneath the surface of his skin. He had never felt the amount of pure scorn he now held for another person in his entire life. Suddenly, he also felt a debilitating weakness that deflated his pride. He realized that no matter how hard he worked or how clean of a life he led, no matter how good he was to people or how much he loved, there were those in this world who would never believe that he was worthy.

When he first reached out his hand to clasp the envelope, his intention was to take it and throw it back into Joseph Daniels's smug face. But once both men's hands were on the envelope, Joseph leaned in close and spoke.

"You and my daughter are done," he commanded.

Malik stared into his eyes, expecting to see the

same coldness that lived in the man's words and actions, but what he saw instead was fear.

Malik saw through the tough exterior and the superiority complex and spied a man who was so afraid of losing his own foothold on the milk and honey of America's promised dream that he had no choice but to beat down those who were right behind him, also reaching up for better. When Joseph released the envelope and stepped away, Malik held on to it. It occurred to him that men like Joseph Daniels owed a debt and up until that moment, no one had made him pay. He lowered his hand to his side, envelope clenched tightly in his palm, and turned to walk away.

"I knew eventually you'd come to see things my way. It takes a smart man to recognize when he is out of his league," Joseph said to Malik's back.

Malik spun around.

"How long are you going to live in your land of make believe, Mr. Daniels? How long are you going to pretend that your money, your education and your luxurious lifestyle negates your blackness?"

"How dare you?"

"No, how dare you? How dare you insult our ancestors by stepping on their backs to get where you and your family are and then acting like you did it all by yourself? Now you disassociate yourself with the very poor, uneducated, working-class black people that paved the way for you.

"Ha." Malik laughed sardonically. "I feel sorry for you, Mr. Daniels, because with all that you have, you are still missing so much. You have one daughter who is doing everything in her powers not to be like you…" Malik's voiced trailed off, the thought of Kennedy still causing him pain.

"Kennedy has more character and integrity in her little finger than you have in your entire self-righteous, shallow body."

"Now that is laughable. You have the nerve to speak to me about integrity," Joseph said.

He glanced down at the manila envelope that Malik clutched in his hands.

Joseph's glare was full of contempt as he looked at Malik for a moment longer, before turning on his heel and walking away. He climbed into his car and drove away, gravel spitting from beneath his tires. It was unclear to either man whether the hatred they felt at that moment was directed toward each other or at themselves.

Chapter 21

The sun caressed Kennedy's face, neck and extremities as she lay on a chaise on the balcony of a suite at Magen's Point Resort on the enchanting island of St. Croix in the Virgin Islands. The sounds of the water lapping against the shoreline soothed her ears and restless heart. The previous night had been a long one, as she tossed and turned on an unfamiliar mattress. She didn't attempt to trick herself into believing that being away from home was the only reason why she was restless. It had been almost two weeks since her breakup with Malik, and with the passing of each day came an even heavier weight on her heart. She had not believed that she would miss him as much as she did, and no amount of fun in the sun was going to fix that.

Coming to the Virgin Islands had been Madison's idea. Having been absolutely desperate to get out from under her mother's watch, Madison had hopped in her car and popped up on Kennedy's doorstep. One look at her sister, who at four o'clock in the afternoon was still lounging in her pajamas, hair a mess and face stained with tears, and Madison realized that whatever she was going through could wait. In a rare show of selflessness, Madison held her sister's hand while she cried. They lay in Kennedy's bed together, talking and crying, and for the first time in a very long time they commiserated over Kennedy's drama as opposed to Madison's.

"Girl, you know how critical Mommy and Daddy are. You could have brought home Jesus Christ himself and they'd have something to say about his sandals or his long hair," Madison lamented.

"That's just it, Maddie. I'm tired of trying to please them. What are we supposed to do? Spend our entire lives living up to their demands?"

"I think that's what they expect, but I for one will be the first to burst their bubble. I'm my own person, and I am not going to allow them to bully me," Madison stated emphatically.

"It's not that easy for me, Maddie. I don't know how to *not* do what they want me to do," Kennedy said.

"Well, maybe you're looking at things the wrong way. Instead trying to not do what they want you to do, how about just *doing* what you want to do, feel me? Now, for starters, why don't you tell me about this guy that's got Mommy and Daddy all worked up?"

Kennedy attempted to talk about Malik. She wanted to explain to her sister how he had ever so gently slipped into her life and her heart, soothing her fears and helping her chart a new course for her life. Unfortunately, she was unable to put those thoughts into words before she was overcome with heartbreaking grief.

"All right, that's it," Madison said, jumping up from the bed. It was well into the middle of the night and they had made their way through a half a gallon of Chunky Chocolate ice cream and a box of macadamia-nut cookies. She padded in bare feet across the bedroom and out into the hallway.

"Where are you going?" Kennedy called after her.

"Just trust me," Madison called back.

Kennedy remained in bed, her eyes suddenly growing heavy from all of the crying she'd done and the lack of sleep. As she lay there, wondering what Madison was up to and reflecting on how good it felt to have her sister there with her, even if it didn't change one thing in her life, she began dozing off. It was only a matter of minutes after her last coherent thought that Madison burst back into the bedroom.

"All right, I'm setting your alarm for eight o'clock in the morning. We've got a twelve noon flight to catch," she announced.

Kennedy kept her eyes closed, certain that she hadn't heard what she thought she'd heard her sister saying. But sure enough, when the alarm began to buzz, Madison ushered her out of bed, helped her gather the bare essentials and a few articles of clothing. Before Kennedy could wrap her brain around what was happening, Muppet had been hustled off to a kennel and they were on a plane to St. Croix.

"Oh, just relax and go along for the ride," Madison said in answer to Kennedy's protests.

Two days later, Kennedy had finally begun to relax and enjoy the hot sand in her toes and the warm waves that crashed against her body. Two beautiful, apparently single women like Kennedy and Madison received a lot of attention on the beach, and, of course, Madison ate it up. Kennedy, while polite, remained reserved, her heart and mind still on Malik.

"This brother must have really put it on you, huh?" Madison remarked after Kennedy turned down a dinner invitation from the frat brothers who were staying at the same resort. "You are whipped."

"Just because I'm not interested in some buff, beach boys doesn't mean that I'm whipped, Madison," Kennedy retorted.

"Mmm, hmm, whatever. I just hope you and this

dude get back together so I can get a chance to meet him. I need to see for myself what the brother's working with." Madison laughed.

"Stop being so nasty, Maddie. I swear, you can be so crass sometimes. Besides, it doesn't really look like there's a chance in hell that Malik and I are going to get back together. Mommy and Daddy would go berserk, anyway."

"Kennedy, would you please grow the hell up and stop running around here trying to be Little Miss Perfect. I mean, damn, at some point Mommy and Daddy are going to be two old geezers who barely remember their own names. What are you going to do then? I'll tell you what, you'll be sitting around on a park bench somewhere feeding the pigeons because you let them stop you from having a shot at a life of your own."

Kennedy shook her head from side to side.

"I'm sure somewhere in that twisted brain of yours, you thought that you were saying something uplifting to me just now, don't you?"

"I'm just telling you like it is. If that man means half as much to you as you say he does, I just don't understand what the problem is. But, hey, you're a grown woman. Do what you want. I know what I'm going to do," Madison said, her eyes and attention trained on a tall, dark-haired man who was standing near the shoreline holding a surfboard.

"I'm going to go over there and get surfing lessons.

Hmph, be still my heart," she said as she dusted the sand off the butt of her skimpy bikini bottom and switched her way down to the water's edge.

There was some merit in what Madison had said. Kennedy could not deny that. She wrestled with the resentment she felt toward Malik and his unwillingness to fight for her. If he loved her, wouldn't he have hung in there despite the resistance from her parents? Wasn't endurance through trials and tribulations a test of love? These questions burned inside of Kennedy and even though she tried to hold on to the anger she felt toward Malik, it was impossible to do. She loved the man and she was just not ready to give up on him. That day Kennedy vowed she would wait for Malik to come to his senses.

Chapter 22

Madison and her surfer dude hit it off famously, so much so that she failed to return to the room she was sharing with Kennedy until the next morning. Kennedy restrained herself from scolding Madison. After all, Madison was over the age of consent. She held her tongue as her sister slipped into the room and headed straight for the shower. When she climbed into the king-size bed next to Kennedy a few minutes later, Kennedy pretended to be asleep.

"Kennedy, are you asleep?" Madison asked after a few moments.

"Yes, why?"

"Nothing. Forget it," Madison said.

Kennedy rolled over to face her sister.

"What's the matter Maddie?" Kennedy asked.

"Nothing's wrong. I just wanted to talk, but if you're asleep—"

"For the love of God, Maddie, spit it out already."

"All right, keep your shirt on. I just wanted to ask you something."

Madison sighed and Kennedy waited patiently in the early morning for her sister to unburden herself.

"How do you know that this Malik guy really loves you? I mean, how do you know when a guy really means it when he says he loves you and is not just running game?"

Kennedy considered her sister's question for a moment.

"I think you know because it's not just about what he says or how or when he says it. Love is something you feel in your spirit. You feel it when a man loves you because it shows in his touch and in his actions. Long before Malik ever said the words to me, I felt it," Kennedy answered.

Madison lay silent for so long that Kennedy thought she had fallen asleep.

"I wonder if that will ever happen for me," Madison said after a long while.

"Oh, it will, Maddie. It will. You just have to be patient and wait on it. It's not something you can plan for or set up. The right man is going to come along and find you. He'll be all yours and when he says he loves you, you'll believe it."

Kennedy moved closer to her sister, pulling her into her arms. She wished that she could take some of the confusion her sister was going through away, but she knew that Madison had to walk her own path through life. Unlike their parents, Kennedy knew that no amount of forced guidance and demands would force Madison to live the life they wanted her to live. She would have to learn for herself that whatever she was looking for would not be found through casual flings with unworthy men. In the meantime, all anyone could do was support her and love her.

Chapter 23

Back in D.C., two relatively uneventful weeks passed as Kennedy attempted to restructure her life without Malik. Kennedy began and ended each day with a prayer hoping that Malik was at peace and asking that, if in God's wisdom he saw fit to bring them back together, neither of them did anything to stand in the way of that.

After days of working on herself, inside and out, she decided it was time to go back to work again because sitting around her apartment licking her wounds was futile. The idea of returning to Morgan Stanley, however, was a bitter pill for her to swallow because in the months since the accident and her departure from the company, she'd come to realize that while she was proud of her success, it had come at a very high cost.

Kennedy had devoted so much of her time and daily energies to becoming a forceful cookie-cut copy of the perfect junior executive that she had sacrificed the simple pleasures in life. It took losing her eyesight for her to see that there was more to life than climbing the corporate ladder and making a name for yourself. It took nearly losing her life to learn that there were more important things to accomplish in one's lifetime than million-dollar corporate mergers. What's more, it was through meeting Malik that she came to understand that at the end of the day, none of those things mattered if you didn't have someone at home who loved you just because.

Right before she called in to make plans to return, be it through divine intervention or fate, she was called upon to put her plans aside and to assist with performing damage control to the Daniels family name…again.

Kennedy received the news that her reckless little sister was in some sort of crisis and her parents were worried sick—both about her and about what people would think of them. Once again, Kennedy got the phone call and was expected to come home without delay. Kennedy responded, as she always did, but this time things were different. This time she went home with her own agenda. It was time to set the record straight with her parents for once and for all.

Madison had left a cryptic note and disappeared for four days, without so much as a phone call. When she'd stumbled home at the end of that period, it was clear to her parents that she'd been binge drinking, again. According to Madison, she was not an alcoholic, and she'd stand up and shout that to anyone who thought otherwise. As far as Kennedy was concerned, that wasn't really even the issue. Madison's major problem was the fact that she was a confused, spoiled little rich girl who'd try anything with anyone, at least once, just for the heck of it. Madison was so caught up in her own turmoil, she had no regard for how her actions would affect those around her, or how they would impact her own life in the long run. Kennedy did not know what it would take for Madison to get her life together and frankly, she was quite tired of even thinking about it. The one thing Kennedy did know, however, was that if her parents stopped smothering Madison, perhaps she would have a chance to come into her own.

Madison needed to take responsibility for her own life and actions, and she could not do that with Mommy and Daddy constantly on her back.

Kennedy was plagued by these thoughts when she arrived at her parents' home. Elmira, never one to let any grass grow under her feet, called Madison down for a family meeting five minutes after Kennedy's car pulled into the driveway. Five minutes after that, sparks were flying and tempers were flaring. Unwilling to fight, Madison tore out of the living room.

"Madison Alexandra Daniels, get back here this instant," Elmira demanded to her retreating back.

"Mother, just leave her alone. God, can't you just back off for five minutes and let her breathe," Kennedy snapped.

"Well, excuse me for caring about my daughters. I thought that was a mother's right," Elmira retorted, her cheeks flushed.

"Caring is one thing. What you do is smothering and you need to stop it right now," Kennedy said.

"All right now, Kennedy, that's your mother you're talking to. Watch your tone," Joseph said.

Both women turned toward the patio doorway, Kennedy following the sound of her father's voice. They didn't know how long he had been there or how much of the argument between the strong-willed Daniels women he had witnessed.

"Look, I'm not trying to be disrespectful, but you guys are going to have to give Madison some breathing room or else you're going to push her away. I know you want what's best for her, but she's a grown woman. You guys standing over her and riding her is not going to help. It's just going to make matters worse."

"Pardon me, Kennedy, but when you have your own children, after you've spent almost three decades being a mother, then you can tell me how to do it. Until then, I'd appreciate if you'd keep your advice to yourself," Elmira spat. "Now, if you don't mind, I'm going to talk to Madison," she huffed as she headed toward the spiral stairway up which Madison had fled.

"No, Mother, you are *not,*" Kennedy countered harshly.

"Kennedy!" Joseph exclaimed. "What has happened to you, young lady? Talking to your mother this way is not acceptable."

"What has happened to me? Let's see, Dad, where should I begin? I damned near died in a car wreck, lost my eyesight…as soon as my bosses stop feeling pity for me I will have lost my job for good and what else? Oh, how could I forget… thanks to your meddling, I've lost the first man I've ever loved, a man who you guys despised. Forgive me if I'm not quite myself," Kennedy said with more venom than she'd ever expressed in her entire life.

Had she taken a moment to think about her words, she probably would have been just as shocked as her parents were that she had spoken to them in that manner. It was as if all the years of listening to their admonishments, all the "Kennedy don't do this" and "Kennedy that's not acceptable," had coming crashing down on her all at once. She was so tired of living their lives that she felt as if she would explode. She did, in fact, explode and the anguish that she'd been surfing through over the split with Malik, was just the catalyst to push her over the edge.

"Kennedy, let's sit down and talk, without all of this yelling. You're upsetting your mother tremendously," Joseph said, after several charged moments.

"No, Dad, I don't want to sit down and talk. For once I want to stand up and, and…shout. I want you guys to listen to what I have to say and to hear me. There is no such thing as perfection. Do you understand that? Both Madison and I are going to make mistakes. Some will be big mistakes and some will be inconsequential, but we're going to make them. I hate to rain on your little parade, but we are not perfect."

"No one ever expected you to be perfect, Kennedy," Elmira said, having finally found her voice.

Kennedy whirled around to the direction from which her mother's voice came. Elmira had moved to the baby grand piano in the southwest corner of the room. She was sitting on the stool, her back to the keys.

"Tell that to Madison up there, who's spent the last five years trying so hard to get you guys to let her be herself that she's damn near lost herself in the process. Do you think she's doing all of these whacky things just for the hell of it? The bottom line, Mother, is that Madison and I are grown and if we make mistakes, they are our mistakes to make. It's time for you guys to back the hell off."

"How dare you! Your father and I have given you everything…every possible advantage in this world. We've made your lives so that you could go anywhere you want, do anything you want and we will not sit idly by and watch either one of you squander that. Not Madison on drugs, alcohol or sordid affairs and not you on some…some—"

"Elmira," Joseph warned.

"No, go ahead, Mother, say it. Some what? Some blue-collar, working-class, didn't go to college bum."

"Kennedy—" Joseph began.

"Don't push me, Kennedy," Elmira said.

"Say it, Mother. Tell me all about how Malik isn't good enough because his father was a doorman and his mother a maid. Why can't you understand that everything about Malik and his family, their hardships and their struggles, have helped to shape him into the caring, compassionate man that he is. Malik is a man whose strength lies not in his financial portfolio or his investment holdings. It's in his impeccable character, his strength of spirit and his morals."

"Spare me," Elmira scoffed.

"No, Mother. It's true. Do you know that Malik is trying to open a community center for kids in his old neighborhood? Basically, while you guys are busy writing monthly checks out to your little laundry list of charities that you and your country club peers deem worthy, he's trying to do something that will really make a difference. I have never met a man more honorable than Malik, and I don't doubt for one minute that I ever will."

"Kennedy, you are too old to be so naive," Elmira said. "Malik Crawford is none of those things."

Kennedy's sardonic laugh shook her body.

"What was that you used to say all the time? 'For God's sake, Kennedy, don't even look at those darkie little boys. Think about your children.' What's the problem, Mother, did Malik not pass the paper bag test? Shoot, Dad, you know you barely made it yourself."

Elmira rushed across the room toward her daughter, snatching her by the shoulders. She shook Kennedy roughly until Joseph jumped up and stepped in between them. It was the first time that Kennedy could ever remember her mother touching her out of anger and part of her was stunned. The other part of her felt as though her mother's behavior was just further proof of how much she wanted to control Kennedy's every thought and emotion.

"You can't make me think your thoughts or live your life. I won't do it anymore," she screamed into her mother's face.

"So what do you want to do, Kennedy? Huh?

What do you want to do? Do you plan on finding that man and begging him to take you back? Is that it? Ha." Elmira laughed, her face contorted. "He doesn't love you, Kennedy. Do you hear me? He does not love you. If he did, he would never have taken twenty thousand dollars from your father."

"Elmira!" Joseph shouted, turning away from Kennedy and facing his wife.

His glare was a mixture of anger and disbelief as he stared at Elmira. He could not believe that she would be as cruel as that, but there was no denying that she'd lost control and had lashed out at Kennedy, hitting her with a truth that she knew would hurt tremendously.

The seconds ticked by in a splintering silence. No one moved or dared to speak. Kennedy stood in between her parents, the silence causing her head to hurt. At that moment, more than any time since the car accident, she wished that she could have the use of her eyes for just one minute. She wanted to look at the faces of her parents, study their expressions and figure out beyond the shadow of a doubt if they were truly the monsters that she was beginning to believe them to be.

"Kennedy, let me explain," Joseph said after an eternity of stillness.

"Mother, what are you talking about?"

Kennedy ignored her father's attempts to pacify her with his calm, even tone. Joseph glared at his wife, willing her mouth shut with his eyes. Elmira stood with her mouth closed, her chin jutting outward defiantly. Her expression was almost smug, but the look that Joseph gave her was enough to wipe most of it off of her face. She did not speak.

"Mother?"

Joseph moved closer to his daughter, placing a hand on her trembling shoulder.

"Kennedy, baby, I'm sorry. I wish things could have gone differently. I would do anything for you not to ever be hurt."

"What exactly does that mean, Daddy? Did you pay him to leave me?" Kennedy asked directly.

"It wasn't like that. I simply…we simply explained to him that you and he were not meant to be. Malik had to be made to understand that you could never be satisfied with a man like him. He was out of his league, and he came to realize that. The money, well the money was just a compensation of sorts for his loss."

Once again Kennedy felt the absence of her vision. The driving wish at that moment was to be able to see with her own eyes her parents' faces. She wanted to see for herself if they had even one iota of remorse. Despite all the things they had ever said or done that she disagreed with, this was by far the most devastating. Accepting that her parents could be as manipulative and immoral as this was an extremely large pill to swallow. In fact, she felt herself about to choke on it.

Kennedy refused to break down in front of them. In fact, she couldn't have even if she wanted to. Coldness spread over her whole body all at once, freezing her heart and stopping the blood flow in her extremities. Later on, she wouldn't remember walking out of the room, retrieving her purse and jacket from the hall chair where she'd laid them when she'd arrived earlier that afternoon and whistling for Muppet, who lay near the lemon tree on the side of her parents' home. She'd have no recollection of walking out of the house, crossing the lawn and walking the quarter of a mile down to the gatehouse, where Mr. Melvin, the guard who received any visitors to the half a dozen houses on Cherry Hill Road, would call her a cab.

By the time the driver pulled into the driveway of Skyy's parents' home, the frost had melted and Kennedy could feel a searing pain in the place where her heart resided. She felt the folded bills in her purse until she found the right combination of tucks and bends in order to pay the fare. Muppet, seeming to sense that his master was fragile, moved slowly up the walk to the front door. Kennedy didn't think she could stand for a minute longer, nearly collapsing into Skyy's arms when her friend opened the door. And then the glacier cracked, separating into a dozen little pieces and Kennedy cried enough tears to saturate the Sahara.

Chapter 24

Malik stared at the manila envelope filled with hundred-dollar bills as if it were a snake ready to spring from the dresser drawer and sting him with its deadly venom. When he first placed the envelope in the bottom drawer of his chest of drawers almost a month before, he'd avoided the drawer like the plague. Although he knew it was not likely, part of him believed that if he didn't look at it or touch it, perhaps he could pretend that it didn't exist. An even further stretch of hope was that if the money didn't exist, none of the past six months of his life with Kennedy existed and it could all be relegated to some dusty corner of a fantasy where pain and longing did not register.

He scratched at the hair that had grown in on his face since his last shave three days before. It had been a three-day weekend for him and he had not ventured out of his apartment. The weather outside was mild and inviting, and he had a million errands to run and tasks that he needed to do. For the past couple of weeks, however, as his tortured mind lived in a constant state of replay, images of Kennedy's face freeze-framed on his brain, he'd opened the drawer a half dozen times. He had yet to summon the courage to touch the envelope.

He had told himself that he had not taken the money as a payoff. Hadn't he known from the very beginning that there would be no happily ever after for him and Kennedy? Of course, his mind had consistently held fast to that unspoken understanding. Yet his heart had leapt forward without hesitation and his soul had united with hers for keeps.

Plans for the community center were progressing at warp speed. The business plan Kennedy had helped him draw up was impeccable and already he had two banks interested in providing funding in the form of low-interest loans. In addition, he'd secured a promise from a computer company to provide computers for the technology lab he envisioned, a major sporting goods chain was on board to provide athletic equipment for the gymnasium at a marked discount and the individuals at the Urban Enterprise Initiative with whom Kennedy had put him in touch were waiting for the green light to aid him in securing state funding. He was negotiating with the city's zoning department over possible spaces for the center to be housed and was confident that a location would be decided upon shortly.

The best part of it all was that Malcolm was down with him, prepared to head the construction on the facility space Malik was about to put an offer on. Having his brother working by his side as he undertook this, his life's work, was more than he could have hoped for. He also prayed that the fact that Malcolm would be able to secure steady income from him for a time would help him get his affairs in line.

Malik's dream was finally coming true after years of scheming, yet the reality of it looked as if it were filmed in black and white instead of the high definition of his imagination. He could not escape the fact that had he not met Kennedy, he would not be this close to bringing the community center to life. That in and of itself was a permanent reminder of how much she had changed his life.

Malik's agonized revelry was interrupted by noises coming from the room his brother was staying in. Malcolm and Nicole, the mother of his first son, were going at it for what he counted to be the third time that night. Nicole was a screamer and the walls of Malik's apartment were no match for her lungs. Malik slammed the drawer shut and walked over to his bed.

He turned out the lamp on the nightstand, lay down on his back and covered his face with a pillow. As he lay he wished he could be more like his brother, who never let anyone get under his skin and into his heart. Yet even as he considered this, Malik knew that he would never want to live Malcolm's life. Loving Kennedy had been the best thing that ever happened to him and losing her was the worst. Even as he hoped that somehow he would be able to move past this time in his life, he knew that the mark Kennedy had left on his heart was stamped in indelible ink. Her strokes on his soul would never be replaced.

Malik realized that his only option was to become a man that Kennedy could proudly call her own and then step to her correctly this time. He would use the Daniels money toward the community center, where it would do something good and positive for people who needed it. Even if Kennedy never took him back, at least she would know that he was not a quitter when it came to accomplishing his goals, no matter how long it took or how difficult it was. He did not allow himself to think about the possibility that it would be too late by the time he found her again.

Chapter 25

Kennedy awoke early on the first morning after her return to D.C. It was raining and she lay motionless with her eyes closed, listening to the sound of the rain as it pelted her bedroom windows. She was tempted to lay there all day, unwilling to face the world on a day that mirrored her dreary mood.

This morning she realized that she couldn't go back to sleep even if she really did want to. Slowly, she opened her eyes as she sat up. There was a difference that caused her to blink once and then twice, as her pulse began to race.

Kennedy took a couple of deep breaths, trying to calm herself down. It had to just be her mind playing tricks on her. Sometimes when a person wanted a thing badly enough, their mind could be tricked into believing that that thing was actually there. The blurred images that she thought were taking shape in front of her could not possibly be there. She closed her eyes again, actually hoping that by the time she opened them again, the images would be gone and the familiar darkness to which she had become accustomed would have returned.

Kennedy threw back the comforter that covered her body. Her long legs swung over the side of the bed and she planted her feet on the floor. She counted down from ten, preparing herself for her daily ritual of counting her steps to the bathroom situated just outside of her bedroom door. Although the hour was early, just after six o'clock in the morning, the room was already bathed in sunlight. She tilted her face toward the window, feeling the warm light on her face. When she opened her eyes again, there was no dismissing or explaining the fact that while she'd slept, there had been a change in her vision.

Stunned, her roaming eyes landed on the armoire directly across from her. The armoire was polished oak. While the image was very fuzzy, she could clearly make out what it was. Her eyes traveled up and down the piece of furniture as she blinked several times to try to bring the blurred shape into focus. At the top of the armoire was a huge stuffed teddy bear Malik had won for her at the carnival they'd gone to.

Kennedy rose from the edge of the bed, her legs trembling as she walked toward the armoire. She reached up and pulled the teddy bear down. She felt along the back of the bear, its beige fur soft and fluffy. She could not see the brown stitched fabric that served as its nose, mouth and paw pads, but she could make out the large black plastic circles that formed its eyes. She lifted the teddy bear up into the air, then down and side to side, following it with her eyes in amazement.

As the reality finally sank in, she hugged the bear to her chest and spun around. Tears sprung to her eyes and slid down her cheeks. She wiped at the moisture quickly, not wishing to have anything obstruct her view to the world. While it was not a complete return to sight, it was a definite improvement. It was what she and the doctors had been waiting for, even when she'd stopped believing in their words of encouragement that it was possible that her vision would return one day.

"Yes!" she exclaimed, causing Muppet to stir from his position at the foot of her bed.

She watched the dog trot over to her side and stop next to her, looking up into her face quizzically. She could make out the dog's soft fur, the wagging tail hazy as it swished from side to side. The joy that bubbled up inside of her was contagious and

Muppet began to do a little dance in which his lower body wiggled with his wagging tail. He barked twice, sharply, and Kennedy reached down to stroke his head. For the first time since she and Muppet had become companions, she did not have to feel along his back or neck to locate the space between his eyes where he liked to be scratched. Her hand landed directly on his head and she rubbed him, her smile beaming as a fresh batch of tears sprang to her eyes.

Eventually, Kennedy made her way back to the bed and lifted the phone onto her lap. She needed to call someone. Her first thought caused her to freeze, her fingers poised over the number pad. She was about to call Malik, having temporarily forgotten the anguish of the past few weeks in her excitement. Once again she was reminded of how much he'd meant to her and how much she'd lost. For the past few months in moments of deep agony and of great elation, Malik had been the person she'd sought to share things with. From the moment they'd met, he'd been there for her, unwavering in his support. Yet that had been shattered and now that he was gone, she was at a loss. She sighed heavily and dialed a number.

"Hello, you've reached Dr. Pitcher's answering service. Is this an emergency?"

"No, it's not an emergency, but can the doctor be paged?" Kennedy asked.

"May I have your name and the nature of your call?" the operator asked.

"My name is Kennedy Daniels, and I'm one of Dr. Pitcher's patients. The message is that there's been a change in my condition, and I'd like to come in for an exam as soon as possible."

"Thank you and is this number you're calling from the best number for him to reach you, Ms. Daniels?"

"Yes, I'm at home. I'll be here all day. Thank you."

Kennedy returned the phone to the cradle, and leaned back against the headboard of the bed. While she waited anxiously for the doctor's call, she thought about calling Skyy, but remembered that her friend was on an early morning flight back to Italy.

Calling her parents was completely out of the question because while she was no longer enraged at what they had done, she was still not ready to talk to them. Madison had enough to deal with and even if she was up to talking to Kennedy, Madison might tell her parents about her call. Sharing good news with them was the last thing she wanted to do right now, especially since her fury had not quite reached the cooling point. The biggest thing that could have happened to her had just occurred and there was not one person whom she could share it with. That made it all the more bittersweet.

Seated that afternoon in Dr. Pitcher's office, Kennedy explained what had occurred from the moment she'd first opened her eyes that morning. In place of the snatches of light and blurred shadows of objects devoid of color, which Kennedy had been limited to seeing for the past five months, were more defined images in which she could distinguish shades of color and shapes.

"Well, let's just take a peek at what's going on," Dr. Pitcher said.

He examined both eyes thoroughly, using a variety of testing devices. Kennedy had been through so much testing since the accident that she knew precisely what he was doing each step of the way. Nevertheless, he explained his actions as if it were her first time.

When he'd finished his tests, Dr. Pitcher's reserved excitement gave Kennedy further encouragement.

"Kennedy, it appears that the PTVS caused by the deceleration of your brain during the crash is re-versing itself. I do have to remind you that since we know so little about this condition, we still cannot predict what degree your sight will ever return. This could be just the beginning of a remarkable, full recovery or—"

"It could be the end…the best that it gets. I know that, Dr. Pitcher. I've been telling myself that all morning, but still…it's more than I've had to hold on to since the accident so I'm going to have a little faith."

"As well you should, young lady. I'd like you to come back in at the end of the week. We'll take another look and see what's happening. In the meantime, give my office a call if there are any other improvements or, if you experience any pain or discomfort. All right?"

"Yes, thanks, Dr. Pitcher."

By the time Kennedy returned home, she was at war with herself. She wanted to call someone, but realized that she really didn't have much to tell. It was bad enough to have *her* hopes pumped up, but to get those who loved her excited before she knew exactly what she was dealing with would be cruel. Besides, the one person that she would have shared her news with she no longer had access to.

In the days that unfolded, Kennedy continued to see improvements in her vision. By the time she returned for her second visit with Dr. Pitcher, she could see bright colors and was able to read the eye chart at the fourth line, although it remained blurry.

"L, P, E, D," she proudly called as Dr. Pitcher pointed from line to line.

This time Dr. Pitcher performed a test to determine the contrast sensitivity in Kennedy's eyes.

"It looks like things are progressing steadily, but you still have a ways to go. Driving is still out of the question because you have a very low contrast sensitivity. That means when driving you would be unable to see traffic lights or spot other cars and pedestrians with dependability."

She was on cloud nine as she left the doctor's office that second day and despite the possibility that she had reached the height of her recovery, she continued to grow more excited and optimistic. She continued to take Muppet everywhere she went, which was a good thing since even when walking down the street, she still could not distinguish between the sidewalk and curbs. None of that mattered, however, because she was getting better with each passing day. Besides, she and Muppet had become best friends and considering how isolated she had begun feeling, she was grateful to have Muppet at her side.

That night Kennedy took herself out to dinner at an upscale restaurant to enjoy her liberation and was able to read much of the menu on her own. She celebrated with a delicately prepared filet mignon and a vintage wine, smiling more in one evening than she had in a long time. For the first time she let herself believe that she would get back to where she once was in her life again, although without Malik in it, she did not know for sure if the past was a place she really wanted to be, anyway.

Chapter 26

"I feel like I'm in somebody's wildest dream," Kennedy said as she looked down over the boot-shaped country of Italy where it dipped into the Mediterranean Sea as the plane prepared for its final descent.

"Well, my dear, let me pinch you so you'll realize that you are very much awake," Skyy said.

"Ouch!" Kennedy exclaimed when Skyy did, in fact, take a piece of the flesh on her left arm between two fingers and squeeze.

She stared out of the window, still reeling over the fact that she could see anything at all, but amazed by the magnificence of what she could behold.

"If Italy is half as beautiful on the ground as it is from up here, I can see why you love it so much," Kennedy breathed dreamily.

"Girl, everything is beautiful to you these days…it's like you're seeing the world for the first time, huh?" Skyy said wistfully.

Kennedy nodded in full agreement with her friend. There was no denying that now that she had been given the gift of sight again, everything that came into her line of view was stunning. She promised herself not to waste one minute with her eyes closed.

When Skyy had called her from Rome a couple of weeks after her vision began to return, Kennedy had been like a balloon about to burst. Skyy had barely said hello before she blurted out her news. Two weeks later, after wrapping up some business obligations, Skyy had hightailed it to D.C. in order to witness this miracle for herself. It didn't take much convincing on Skyy's part to persuade Kennedy to travel back to Italy with her and as the plane landed, she thanked her friend for knowing intuitively how beneficial taking a trip like this would be for her right now.

They landed in Latium and spent four days in Rome at one of the most beautiful villas in the city. Villa Torlonia, which had recently undergone a major restoration project, was one of the last examples of Roman cultural patronage. The gardens boasted seventeenth-century grace and the grounds were adorned with vintage statues and lamps. The Casino Nobile hosted an exhibition of the Roman School that was a showing of over one hundred works of artists who lived and worked during World Wars I and II. Kennedy had to struggle to keep her jaw from dropping every time she entered a different room or area of the property, so breathtakingly stunning everything was.

Skyy had to drag Kennedy away from Rome kicking and screaming, giving her assurances that the rest of Italy would be equally as captivating. They traveled up north to Lombardy, where they spent two days at Venice at Abano Terme, one of the many spas that have developed on the slopes of the Euganei Hills. There, the volcanic highlands had an abundance of areas where hot water springs gushed out. Skyy introduced Kennedy to mud therapy. The treatments were highly recommended for rheumatic illness and problems with the respiratory and female genital organs. While she had none of those problems, she left Abano Terme feeling as if she had been given a brand new body.

In Milan, Kennedy learned that Skyy had had an ulterior motive when offering to be her tour guide to Italy. It seemed that Samage Designs had an opening for a person to handle the project finance planning for the company and little Ms. Busybody, a.k.a. Skyy Reynolds, had pitched Kennedy's credentials to the company. The very day they arrived in Milan, Kennedy was seated before one half of the namesake, Keith Samage, and was discussing her qualifications. When he made an offer, it was a tongue-tied Kennedy who requested a couple of weeks to consider the unexpected but greatly appreciated opportunity.

Every day they ate traditional Italian meals, starting with breakfast, which was usually *colazione* and cappuccino. Lunch was the big meal of the day for many Italians, consisting of antipasto as a start, a pasta, rice or soup next, followed by a meat or fish served with vegetable or salad. By the time they reached the fresh fruit and the espresso, Kennedy would be ready to fall out of her seat. That did not stop her, however, from enjoying a scrumptious dinner, topped off with one of the hundreds of flavors of Italian ice cream.

They visited Florence and traveled south to Naples. There, Kennedy viewed the archeological sites of Paestum and Velia, falling deeper in love with the country with each day. When they reached Sicily, where they were to spend their last few days, Kennedy knew that she had a very big decision, indeed, to make.

She also learned that there was more than business and the love of the country that had kept her best friend on this side of the globe for the better part of the past year. Salvatore Giuliano, a painter who lived just outside of the city of Palermo, was a dark Sicilian man who was soft-spoken and mild-mannered. He treated Kennedy warmly and with genuine hospitality during their stay at the small villa he owned with his brother, Francesco. Although Skyy divulged little information, the way he held Skyy by the elbow lightly or touched the small of her back intimately told Kennedy all that she needed to know. She was happy for her friend, but secretly wondered if she, too, would have to cross the globe in order to find the man of her dreams.

Chapter 27

"Girl, I'm telling you, you are going to absolutely love living in Italy. Getting away from all the crap you've been dealing with in this stale-assed Chocolate City will make you'll feel like you've died and gone to heaven," Skyy said.

"I hope so, because life here *has* been a little hellish lately," Kennedy remarked. "I'm just concerned about the job. I mean, all I've ever done is money, analyzing financial data and overseeing the money aspects of projects. This job is such a departure from all of that, I don't know if I'll be any good at it."

Kennedy was having a hard time digesting all that had happened in just a short time. Her dream vacation in Italy had turned into a whirlwind job interview, followed by a rapid decision to move there and subsequent uprooting of her life.

"Obviously, Keith thinks you will be or he would never have given you the job. And what's so different about what you'll be doing? You're good with numbers, you have a vision, no pun intended, for making projects come to life from a financial perspective and you're a workaholic."

"Correction. I *was* a workaholic. No more of that. I made it perfectly clear to Keith that my eighteen-hour days were a thing of the past. I have no intentions of putting down roots in Italy. I'm going to travel and see the world. And I need to get back stateside often enough to keep up with Madison. I took this job on the condition that we deal with one project at a time. No promises on either side. He said he was cool with that."

"He's a man of his word. But, I have to tell you, you may be the one who falls in love with a new country and a new job and never want to leave. You see what happened to me," Skyy said.

Kennedy threw a hand on one hip and shot her friend a disturbed look.

"Okay, maybe not a good example. Look at it this way, Kennedy. It'll give you a chance to put some space between your family and you, which you definitely need. I love Elmira like she was my own Mama, but you've got to admit that she can be a bit much. You need some time to be with Kennedy and figure out what you want out of life without anyone else sticking their big noses into your business. And, I know you don't like to talk about *him,* so I won't mention *his* name, but the time away will help you to get him out of your system. If that's in fact what you want to do."

"What do you mean, if that's what I want to do? It's over between Malik and me, period. I've had to accept that because that's the way things are. There's no use crying over what's done, is there?"

"Yeah, that's what your mouth says, but Kennedy, my dear, your actions say something entirely different. You're not dating. You're not even looking. That tells me that the man is far from being out of your system."

"It's strange because when I really think about it, I realize that I didn't even know Malik for very long. I mean, we didn't have time or the ability to do all the things that couples usually do. Because of my blindness, we never went to a movie, never rode bicycles or even saw a concert together. We spent most of our time sitting in my apartment talking. I mean, how do I know that I really even knew the man?"

"Kennedy, you're the only one who can say how well you knew him. You've got to search your heart and determine that one for yourself. From the outside looking in, I can tell you that whatever it was you had going on with brother man, it was deep and it left a major impression on you."

"Yeah, kinda like the measles." Kennedy laughed sarcastically.

"Now there's a greeting card. Catching love is like catching the measles," Skyy said and laughed, too.

"You know something, Skyy, I've got to be honest. I wholeheartedly believed that it was my parents' interfering and the constant weight of their opinionated commentaries that ruined my relationship with Malik, but I don't believe that anymore," Kennedy admitted.

"No?"

"No. I mean, their meddling didn't help, but—"

"Yeah, and his taking that money from your father didn't help things, either," Skyy reminded.

"Very true, but perhaps if I had had more faith in him and in us, I would have stood up to them from the get-go and avoided all of that in the end," Kennedy said.

Skyy chewed on her friend's words for a moment without speaking.

"Don't tell me you're getting wise on me in your old age," she remarked at last.

"What? Please, you know I've always been wise. That's why you hang out with me—hoping some of it rubs off on you. No, what I've gotten is even wiser, as if that's possible," Kennedy joked.

"Uh oh, look at you. You've got your sense of

humor back along with your eyesight. Watch out now," Skyy teased.

"Stop trying to analyze me and help me pack the rest of this stuff," Kennedy said, tossing a roll of heavy-duty adhesive tape toward Skyy.

"Who the heck is this chick you're subletting to, anyway? Shoot, I don't see why we can't just stick all of your belongings in the spare bedroom, lock the door and be done with it."

"Spoken like a woman who has never officially moved out of her parents' home."

"No need to get nasty, Miss. All right, let's hurry this up, though, because I want to go out tonight. There's a new band playing at The Dive and we are going to be in there," Skyy answered.

"Why do you know more about the social scene in my state than I do?" Kennedy questioned.

"Because unlike you, I haven't been so occupied by love that I've shut myself off from the world."

"Skyy—" Kennedy warned.

"My lips are sealed," Skyy said, making a mock showing of zipping her lips.

A few minutes later, with a look that said she was about to burst at the seams, Skyy made one final comment.

"You need to see him one more time, before you leave for Italy. You owe it to yourself, Kennedy."

Kennedy let Skyy's words hang in the air. The

only sound was the crumpling of newspaper as they wrapped her breakables and loaded them into waiting cardboard boxes.

Chapter 28

As Kennedy dressed hurriedly, the telephone rang. She knew that it was her mother yet again, calling from the hotel to find out what was taking Kennedy so long. She pulled a yellow cashmere sweater over her head as she walked toward the kitchen where the only phone that hadn't been packed away remained.

"Yes, Mother," she said, snatching up the receiver.

She pointed the remote control toward the living room and pressed mute on the television at the same time.

"Kennedy, it's getting late. Are you all right, dear?"

"Yes, Mother. I'm just running a little behind, but I'll be there soon. Where are Dad and Madison?"

"They're right here. Honey, why don't you let us come to you. We can pick you up and perhaps have dinner at that nice little place up the street from your apartment."

"No, Mother. We're eating at the hotel. I don't need you to come and pick me up. Now, I'm walking out of the door right now. I'll be there in twenty minutes. Bye." Kennedy hung up before her mother could protest further.

It was going to be quite a surprise for her family when she shared her big news with them. She had held on to the secret for long enough. It had been six weeks since she'd first had a return of function in her eyes and in that time, her eyesight had improved even more. The progress she was making was steady and now that she was confident that it was, in fact, going to continue to improve until she was able to live a normal life again, she wanted them to know.

The second bombshell she was about to drop on them would probably not go over as well. She'd met with her bosses at Morgan Stanley the day before and after thanking them for all the support and consideration they'd given her over the past half a year and during her entire tenure at the company, she presented her letter of resignation. They understood her decision to explore different avenues and told her that they would always have a place for her if she changed her mind. Now that that cat was out of the bag, she knew that she had to tell her parents before someone else opened their mouths.

It was not that she had waited until the last minute to tell them out of fear of their reaction or any attempt at changing her mind. She genuinely did not care what they thought about her decision. She had finally reached a place in her life where she was determined to live on her own terms and under her own principles. However, what did bother her was the fact that despite their faults they were a loving family and she knew instinctively that she would be missed.

As she raced past the muted television, something on the screen caught Kennedy's eye. She had been so used to not even looking at the television for the past months, she didn't know what drew her attention to it. It must have been the bold words that read *Community Center* in the middle of the screen. She stopped and turned up the volume.

"Sources say that this new community center will be far different from any of its kind in the country. It will offer a wide variety of services to kids and young adults. According to the director, Mr. Malik Crawford, everything will be free of charge to youth in the Northwest community. The ribbon-cutting ceremony is scheduled for this Saturday at twelve noon and there will certainly be a huge turnout of interested kids and their parents. Back to you in the studio," the reporter announced.

Stunned, Kennedy stared at the television until her cell phone began ringing. Without even looking at it she knew that it was her mother calling again. She snatched her purse from the table and dashed out of the apartment, her mind still focused on what the news program had just reported.

Dinner was a joyous celebration. Elmira's tears of joy at Kennedy's recovery caused her mascara to run and Joseph ordered champagne for the entire restaurant. Surprisingly, when Madison raised her glass to toast, it was filled with sparkling water. Kennedy did not comment on this, simply accepting the fact that she was not the only one who wanted to make some changes in her life.

The biggest surprise of the evening was that when she told her family about her job in Italy and plans to travel, they seemed to be genuinely happy for her. Her father congratulated her on her adventurous spirit and her courage. After dinner, when Elmira asked that Kennedy take a walk with her, she was certain that Elmira's happiness had been false and her true feelings were about to be unleashed. She steeled herself for an argument.

"What's up, Mother?" Kennedy asked as they strolled down the street, passing shops that were now closed, their windows darkened.

"I just wanted to tell you that I'm really proud of you, Kennedy. The way you've dealt with everything. Well, I'm just proud," Elmira said.

She looped her arm through Kennedy's and they continued strolling in silence for a while.

"I also need to say something to you that I don't often say. I guess I'm learning a little in my old age."

Elmira stopped walking and turned to face her daughter. They were standing under the bright lights of a twenty-four-hour Internet café and coffee shop. She reached out and picked a piece of lint from Kennedy's hair.

"I want to apologize to you for all of the awful things I said and did. I have no excuse other than the fact that I love you. A mother's job is to protect her children and sometimes we believe that we're doing what's best for them, when in reality all we're doing is meddling and hurting them."

"Wow, Mother, this is almost too much for me. First I get my eyesight back, now this," Kennedy joked.

"Kennedy—"

"Just teasing, Mother. I appreciate your apology. I guess now is the perfect time to tell you one more little bit of news."

Kennedy filled Elmira in on what she'd just learned about Malik's new community center.

"He worked so hard to get that place for the kids. I'm so proud of what he's been able to accomplish."

Kennedy paused, taking a deep breath before continuing.

"Before I leave for Italy, I need to see him. I need to tell him how proud I am and, well, a few other things."

"So what are you going to do, Kennedy? Track this man down and throw yourself at his feet?"

That was precisely the reaction she expected from her mother.

"Yes, Mother. That's exactly what I'm going to do. I love Malik."

Elmira studied her daughter's face for a moment, having a hard time believing that the words she'd just heard had really come out of her mouth.

"You've really grown up," Elmira said at last.

"Yes, Mother, thanks to you, I'm a grown woman now and I've got to live my life on my terms."

"You're absolutely right. I guess I should have seen this coming…you were always so independent, so inquisitive." Elmira sighed. Elmira's eyes glazed as she was suddenly transported to a time that had long since vacated her everyday thoughts.

"You know, when I first met your father, my parents didn't really approve of him."

"Daddy? Why not?"

"Well, he was premed at a small college in Savannah, Georgia. We met at my first society ball. I was a young debutante and there were about twenty of us girls all coming out. Anyway, your father was the second cousin of the one of the girls. Marjorie Walton. He was her escort."

"Was it love at first sight?"

"For me it was, but things were different then. There were rules and a certain way things were done. His father first spoke to my father and then he met with my parents. All this before he and I had an opportunity to say more than a couple of words to one another. My parents were concerned about his future. His father was a minister down in Georgia and, well, back then ministers were respected as men of God, but they weren't a part of the upper class. So my parents initially discouraged me from dating him and it wasn't until a few years later, when he was a young surgical resident at a small hospital, that they finally gave their approval. He'd proven to be a diligent, driven man and once they got to know him, they loved him as much as I did."

Elmira took Kennedy's hands in hers.

"Your father told me to back off…when we first met Malik, he warned me that I should leave you alone and let you live your life. I guess he could see things clearly long before I could or was willing to. Is he really the one for you, sweetie?"

Kennedy considered her mother's question with the seriousness it deserved.

"There is an empty abyss where he should be in my life, Mommy. Yes, he is the one," she said at last.

Elmira nodded, understanding what her daughter was feeling.

"And he's a good man, this Malik Crawford, isn't he?"

"Yes, Mother, he is. He is amazing. He's courageous and strong. He's giving and selfless."

"Well, as long as he is good to you, what more could a mother ask? But tell me, how do you plan to win Malik back from halfway around the world?"

"I'll worry about all of that later. Right now, I just need to tell him how I feel. He may not even want to hear what I have to say."

"If he doesn't, then he's a damn fool. You, my dear, are a Daniels woman and any man would be lucky to have you on his arm," Elmira pinched Kennedy's cheek. "I meant what I said, honey. I'm so sorry for getting in the way of things. Can you forgive me?"

"Already have, Mother."

The women embraced and for the first time in a long time Kennedy felt a closeness from understanding that she had never shared with her mother before.

Chapter 29

Kennedy stood at the back of the open room, partially obstructed by the large potted tree positioned a few feet behind the last row of white folding chairs. She spotted a man whom she instantly knew was Malik, laying eyes on him for the first time ever.

He was standing near the podium, talking to two other men. If asked, she would not have been able to explain how in a room filled with over a hundred people she had been able to pick him out without one iota of doubt. Perhaps she would have said that when someone has become a part of your very soul, you don't need vision to recognize them.

Malik was as tall as she had imagined, his shoulders as broad as they had felt when she laced her arms around them. He'd grown a beard that covered the smooth cheeks that used to press against her own as they cuddled and read from the same book in bed. He was wearing a sweater that defined his muscular biceps and toned midsection well. Black slacks covered powerful thighs. His skin was every bit as dark as her mother had informed her it was. Rich, dark and as smooth as chocolate. One of his companions said something to him that prompted a smile, and sensuous lips parted revealing startling white teeth. His body shook with laughter and even though she was a hundred feet away, in her mind she heard the resonance of his deep voice. She remembered how many times the sound of his laughter had triggered her own. At long last she was finally able to see how physically magnificent the man whose glorious spirit she'd already enjoyed actually was. At that same moment, she also realized that it really would not have mattered what he looked like because theirs was an attraction that, due to the circumstance of their meeting, had transcended the surface.

Malik stepped away from his companions and stepped onto the stage. He stood in front of the podium and slowly the room grew silent. Once he had the attention of the audience, he smiled that million-dollar smile again and began to speak. She shuddered at the sound of his voice, remembering the very first time she'd heard him speak when she

was still an intensive care patient bruised and
bandaged from head to toe.

"Ladies and gentlemen, first off, I'd like to thank
you all for being here today. Over the past few
weeks as we were planning the program for today's
ribbon-cutting ceremony, people kept asking me
who I was going to invite to be here today. For a
while I was stumped because people were telling
me that I needed to have the press and I needed to
make sure the politicians showed up. They told me
that it was important to have the money folks in the
house…you know, the banks and whatnot. But I
knew that while all of those individuals were important, there were people who were even higher up on
the guest list. People who without their presence,
there would be no reason to cut that ribbon and
open those doors. You guys. You guys are the
children and the parents who this community center
will serve. You are the reason I'm here, you're the
reason why this building is standing. You are the
reason why the money guys are here, why the press
is here and why the politicians are here."

There was a thunderous round of applause.
Malik paused, pulled at his beard with his index
finger and thumb, before continuing.

"This is your center. It belongs to each and every
one of you. My vision is that it provide a refuge. We
all know what's going on out there in those streets.
But parents, I'm promising you right here and right

now, on the record, that none of that nonsense will go on inside of these walls. When your kids are in here, they are safe. When they're on their way here or on their way back home, I'm gonna make sure that they are safe. You and I together are going to do that."

The crowd broke into another round of applause, punctuated by a few shouts of amen. Malik held the crowd in a stupor with the promise of his words as well as the passion in his tone.

"Inside these walls, anyone who enters will be given the opportunity to relax and to learn. They'll be able to be productive, to make plans for their futures and to socialize and be entertained. Together, as a community, we will prove that it's not about where you come from, but about where you're headed. A friend once told me that the difference between a successful kid and a kid who gets lost to the streets is that one of them stopped dreaming. Ladies and gentlemen," Malik raised a pair of scissors over the large red ribbon and sign that rested on an easel next to the podium. As he positioned the scissors to cut the ribbon, he continued, "I give you Kennedy's Kids Community Center, a place for dreams. Thank you."

The crowd exploded in raucous applause, rising to their feet in exuberance. Malik had been absolutely right when he said that a project like this was precisely what the community needed. People needed a place to send their kids where they could believe that they would be safe, protected and respected. Malik's dream was the same dream shared by all of the people present today and seeing it come to fruition was as rewarding for Kennedy as it was for him. She clapped louder and longer than everyone else, her pride overflowing.

"Well, now, I finally see why that man's got you so caught up. What a way with words and certainly not hard on the eyes," Skyy whispered as she sidled next to Kennedy.

"Skyy, you made it," Kennedy said, kissing her friend on the cheek.

"Yeah, girl. Traffic was a bear but I got here just as he took the stage. I was standing back by the door. Mmm, mmm, mmm…that man is fine, Kennedy."

"I know. I mean, I knew he was good-looking even when I couldn't see him. I could just tell, but I really didn't know he was that damned fine."

"Well, now you know. Have you spoken to him yet?"

"No, I'm starting to think that maybe this isn't the right time and place for this."

"Are you crazy? Kennedy, there is no other time. You two have lost too much time as it is, thanks to your nosy-assed parents. Baby girl, I know you're scared, but you are going to have to shake that off, march yourself over there and talk to him. Tell him how you feel and see what happens."

"That's what I'm afraid of, the see what happens part. What if he's over it, Skyy? What if we didn't mean as much to him as we did to me? I'd be mortified…in front of all these people."

"No, you won't. You and I will walk out of here, the divas that we are, with our heads up, booties swaying and to hell with him. If he's stupid enough to let a dime like you walk out of his life, then you don't need him, anyway."

Kennedy weighed Skyy's words in her mind, and while there was undeniable logic in them, she couldn't shake the anxiety that was mounting inside. She decided that she didn't care what pearls of wisdom Skyy dropped on her, she was not ready to face Malik. Deciding to step out as her own woman on her own terms was one thing. This was an entirely different test of character and she had begun to doubt that she could hold up her end. She turned to walk toward the exit but was stopped in her tracks by a voice that she would have recognized immediately out of a crowd of thousands.

"Kennedy?" Malik called.

She turned around slowly to face him. He was less than ten feet away from her and was closing in fast. He wore a puzzled expression, as if he were trying to figure out whether or not his eyes were playing tricks on him.

"Malik," Kennedy responded in a small voice.

"Guess I'll give you two a minute," Skyy said, excusing herself.

Neither Kennedy nor Malik acknowledged her.

Kennedy nervously pushed her shades up farther onto the bridge of her nose. She looked at him through the tinted lenses, acutely aware of the rush of her blood pounding in her ears. Malik moved closer, until he was a mere few inches away from her. He stared at her eyes, gazing through the lenses, his own eyebrows knotted in a perplexed position. Without speaking, he reached out and slid the shades from her face. Kennedy blinked, her eyes focused directly on his.

"You can see me," he said emphatically.

"I always could," Kennedy replied.

Malik searched her face, coming to rest once again on her eyes. They were the same eyes that he'd stared into, drawn in by their dazzling color and wishing they could look back into his. It was at that moment that he admitted the one thing to himself that he had been trying to deny for the past two months. He could not live his life without her.

"Kennedy, I've wanted to call you. I just didn't know what to say to you," Malik began.

"I know. Me, too. I came here today to apologize to you, Malik…for the way my parents treated you and for the way I treated you."

"You? You don't have anything to apologize to me for, Kennedy. I never meant to hurt you. You're the last person in the world I'd ever want to hurt. I just didn't have enough faith."

"Malik, you weren't the only one who lacked faith. By allowing my parents to dictate for all these years every friendship, every love and every single one of the choices I made, I was guilty of everything they were. I always thought that I was so different, but I've taken a long look at myself, Malik, and I realized that by not standing up for myself and my own beliefs, by allowing someone else's prejudices and expectations to dictate my own, I was just like them. So, yes, I do owe you an apology for expecting you to stand up for us when I didn't."

"Kennedy, I just want you to know I did not leave you for your father's money," Malik said.

"I know that."

"I quit on us because I didn't feel worthy of you. I thought that you'd be better off with someone more like you and so would I. Then, afterward, when your father came to me again…well, I figured why not use his money to do something for the people he couldn't even see because his nose was so high up in the air? I thought it would be payback for him taking you away from me to use his money for this place. But that was stupid because he didn't take you away from me. I did that to myself."

Kennedy studied his anguished expression, wanting to reach out and stroke away the lines on his face.

"I should not have taken his money," Malik continued. "I know that now. It didn't matter what the motivation behind it was. By taking it I became exactly what your father believed me to be."

"Malik, he was wrong about you. I know you didn't leave me for my father's money, but because of it."

"Kennedy, I love you so much it hurts me. I have never felt like this for anyone…about anything in my whole life, and I know I'll never feel this way again. But I can't ask you to go against your family. They love you, and I know that you would be miserable without them in your life."

"Malik, are you as blind as I was? I love you too and I'm not going to live without you. Don't you understand that this thing is bigger than my parents, bigger even than you and me separately? We can't just let it die because some antiquated elitist rules say we shouldn't be together. You are a greater man than any blue-blooded, aristocrat with a pedigree two miles long could be."

Malik started to protest. All of the reasons why he shouldn't love her and she shouldn't love him coursed through his brain but not one of them was strong enough to suppress the knowledge that she completed him. Grasping the back of her head, his hand tangled in the soft flowing mane that had once been a place of refuge for him, he pulled her mouth to his. They were oblivious to the smiles and stares around them as they lost themselves in the wonder of their kiss.

"Well, it's about damned time that you two got yourselves together," Skyy chirped, interrupting their reunion. "That's what I'm talking about. Now, break it up and, Malik, get back to work. You've got all these folks standing around here waiting for you to get this show on the road."

The trio laughed. Kennedy introduced her best friend to her man, glad to finally be able to acknowledge to the world that she'd found a man who loved her for who she was and whom she respected as a man who stood for something other than material worth.

Kennedy was proud that she had finally come to know that she was not a person who allowed prejudice and preconceived notions about how people are and how they should be, to dictate her life or love. She had always wondered if she were, in fact, strong enough to step outside of the boundaries of her parents' beliefs and her upbringing to love for the sake of love.

Finally, she knew that she was. Through Malik she had come to know herself and she was rewarded by the fact that she was a person who appreciated the beauty of all people, no matter where they came from or what their last name was.

Epilogue

One year later, Malik and Kennedy exchanged vows in the hills of the countryside of Sicily. Skyy and Salvatore, who were now officially engaged, themselves, served as their witnesses. The ladies wore simple white sundresses and the men, cotton pants and tops. The Daniels' wish for them to have a country club wedding was denied, yet the couple acquiesced to allowing them to throw a huge reception at their estate when the newlyweds returned stateside. The gift and letter sent by them made Kennedy cry tears of joy for a change.

Malik had changed, as well, realizing that true love is worth fighting for, no matter who or what the opponent. He had allowed the Daniels to decide for him his worth as a man and as Kennedy's partner, and almost rob him of the best thing that ever happened to him. As he danced that night under the stars with his new wife, Malik realized that Kennedy had forced him to become the man he'd always wanted to be.

* * * * *

*Don't miss more drama from
Kennedy's baby sister as Madison Daniels
continues her wild ways, but finally meets
a man who can tame her in
FOREIGN AFFAIR
by Kim Shaw
Available in March 2008*

Wanted: Good Christian woman

ESSENCE BESTSELLING AUTHOR

Jacquelin THOMAS

The Pastor's Woman

New preacher Wade Kendrick wants a reserved, traditional woman for a wife—but he only has eyes for Pearl Lockhart, aka Ms. Wrong. Pearl aspires to gospel stardom and doesn't fit into the preacher's world. But their sexual chemistry downright sizzles. What's a sister to do?

THE LOCKHARTS
THREE WEDDINGS AND A REUNION
FOR FOUR SASSY SISTERS, ROMANCE CHANGES EVERYTHING!

Available the first week of September wherever books are sold.

KIMANI ROMANCE™

**The follow-up to *Sweet Surrender*
and *Here and Now*...**

Straight to the **Heart**

Bestselling author

MICHELLE MONKOU

Fearful that her unsavory past is about to be exposed,
hip-hop diva Stacy Watts dates clean-cut Omar Masterson
to save her new image. But their playacting backfires
when their mutual attraction starts to burn out of control!
Now Stacy must fight to keep the secrets of her past
from destroying her future with Omar.

*Available the first week of September
wherever books are sold.*

Grown and sultry...

CANDICE POARCH

As a girl, Jasmine wanted Drake desperately, but Drake considered his best friend's baby sister completely off-limits. Now Jasmine is all grown up, and goes to work for Drake, and he's stunned by the explosive desire he feels for her. Even though she still has way too much attitude, Drake finds himself unable to resist the sassy, sexy beauty....

Available the first week of September wherever books are sold.

Essence bestselling author

DONNA

She's ready for her close-up...

Moments Like This

Part of the Romance in the Spotlight series

Actress and model Dominique Laws has been living the Hollywood dream—fame, fortune, a handsome husband— but lately good roles have been scarce. Then she learns that her business-manager husband has been cheating on her personally and financially. Suddenly, she's down and out in Beverly Hills. But a chance meeting with a Denzel-fine filmmaker may offer the role of a lifetime....

Available the first week of September, wherever books are sold.

ARABESQUE®
www.kimanipress.com

KPDH0190907

National bestselling author

KIM LOUISE

Ever Wonderful

When his truck hits Ariana Macleod's prized Angus,
Braxton Ambrose goes to work on her ranch to
repay her. Handsome Brax's presence feels very
welcome to Ariana—especially when their mutual
attraction explodes into a sizzling affair. Brax isn't the
settling-down type, but when tragedy strikes, he's
determined to convince Ariana that he'll be
with her for the long haul.

"Heartbreaking, heartwarming and downright funny,
this story will totally captivate any reader from
beginning to end."
—*Romantic Times BOOKreviews* on
True Devotion

**Available the first week of September,
wherever books are sold.**

ARABESQUE®

www.kimanipress.com   KPKL0180907